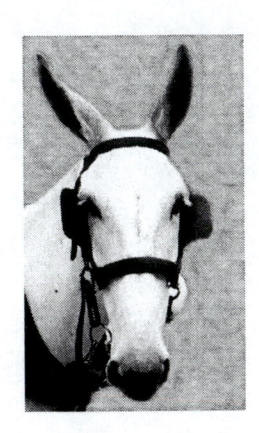

the Old
Family Farm

The Old Family Farm
farm life 100 years ago

George Grier

the Publishers@TreeHouse

©2001 by George Grier

All rights reserved. No part of this book may be reproduced or transmitted in any form or by any means, electronic, digital or mechanical, including photocopying, recording, or by any informational storage or retrieval system without the written permission of the author or his agents except where permitted by law.

Published by the Publishers@TreeHouse,
2658 Patapsco Rd., Finksburg, MD 21048

Printed at Berryville Graphics Westminster

Book design by Phil Grout

Library of Congress Control Number: 2001087705

ISBN 0-9708816-1-4

This book is a work of fiction. Names, characters, places and incidents are either a product of the author's imagination or are used fictitiously. Any resemblance to actual persons, living or dead, events, or locales is entirely coincidental.

To the Carroll County Farm Museum, an institution created to preserve the lifestyles of the old family farm in the 18th and 19th Centuries. May the stories in this book aid in fulfilling its purposes and objectives.

Acknowledgements

The research done for the stories and pictures used in this book involved a great number of helpful people and institutions for which I am grateful. To read back into time and obtain the flavor and accuracy of farm activities of the 1900 era, I have a special thanks to give to **John Crowl**, who along with his immediate families before him, were very active farmers. John's remembrances of their sayings and life experiences are scattered throughout the book.

We learned to rely upon and appreciate the work of three other persons who read the individual stories and made their comments on appropriateness as well as editorial accuracy. They are **Helen Totura, Mary Bruff and Dottie Freeman**, administrator of the Carroll County Farm Museum.

In the back of this book, we have listed the credits (by page number) for pictures which we have been allowed to use throughout the book. We wish to thank those individuals and institutions for their tremendous contribution.

In initiating our project, we interviewed an unusual number of citizens of Maryland and Pennsylvania who were farmers or grew up on farms back in the early 1900s. In the hope of not missing any one person (we apologize if we have inadvertently not given due credit) we thank those persons listed below:

Paul Hering	Howard Leister	Ralph Walsh
John Hull	Royer Shipley	Mr. & Mrs. Stuart Leister
Stoner Fleagle	Homer deGroff	Martin Zimmerman
Raymond Spangler	Earl Beard	Mr. & Mrs. Paul Brauning
Ralph Dinterman	Mildred Stine	Donald Folk
Frank Hull	George Fritz	Dick Reese
Hazel Bixler	Ralph Schuchart	Mr. & Mrs. Jim Caulford
Clint Richards	Robert Basler	Mr. & Mrs. Kenneth Baust
John Carbaugh	Carroll Wilhide	Mr. & Mrs. Jim Shriver
John Totura	Stephen King	Mr. & Mrs. Jean J. John
Elmer Myers	Rodney Haines	Mr. & Mrs. Ralph Dutterer
William Newman	Glenn Haines	Mr. and Mrs. John Elmer Smith
Sen Charles Smelser	Marker Lovell	Mr. and Mrs. Roger Roop
J. Norman Graham	Stanley B. Sutton	Mr. and Mrs. Charles Smith
Dr. Arthur Peck	Judy Stuart	Mr. & Mrs. Donald Dell
Senator Jim Clark	Gerry Bitzel	Mr. & Mrs. Vernon Wolfe
Henry Holloway	Robert Jones	H. Gordon Garrett

(cont'd)

We worked very closely with a number of institutions, particularly relating to picture content. We wish to thank the following:

The University of Maryland (McKeldin Library)	Anne Turkos
Maryland Historical Society	Mary Markey
Historical Society of Carroll County	Jay Graybeal
Historical Society of Harford County	Marlene Magness
Cumberland County PA Historical Society	Richard Tritt
York Heritage Trust	Anne Lloyd
Maryland State Archives	Rob Schoeberlein
Western Maryland College	Joyce Muller
Frederick County Library	Mary Cramer
Frederick News Post	Myra Anderson
Frederick County Historical Society	
Schwenkfelder Museum	
Enoch Pratt Library	
Rose Hill Manor Park	
Hanover Historical Trust	
The Lutheran Seminary	
U.S. Library of Congress	
Nova Development Corp.	
Chelsea House Publishers	

We want to extend a special note of thanks to a rising young artist, **Sarah Brunst,** for an artist rendition of an old family farm which appears on page 7. We wish to applaud the efforts of **Phil Grout** for his work and that of his publishing firm, the Publishers@TreeHouse, in making the design of this book interesting and one easy to read and enjoy. And our appreciation also goes to **John McClurken** of Berryville Graphics who made a special effort to print an attractive book with that company's new "print-on-demand" facility at Random House, Inc. in Westminster, MD.

Foreword

Dear Folks,

    My name is George Shaffer. I was 100 years old on September 14, 1994.

    It's true. I've lived in three centuries—the 19th, 20th and now the 21st.

    Of course, I lived on a farm all my life, and I have a story to tell you about my early days when I was growing up on the old family farm.

    It wasn't always easy. There were no telephones, no radio, no television, no automobiles, trucks, tractors or airplanes—just a lot of plain hard work, even when I was a kid.

    You know, I was called "Young George" from the time old Doc Hering delivered me on that dark night in September 1894 out on my Grandpa Shaffer's farm until I was married.

    I think you'll like to read these stories about my early years as a farm boy.

                                     George Shaffer

Preface

This book deals with the life of a family living and working on a farm during hard times and good, in the late 1800s and early 1900s. The setting can fit most anywhere in the northern Maryland, southern Pennsylvania countryside. The farm activities of the Shaffer family are typical of most farming families in America during that period.

The fictional story focuses on a boy named Young George Shaffer—from the time he was born until his late teen years. The story also includes the lives of his Grandpa, Grandma, Papa and Mama as well as his sisters and a host of neighbors. It is intended that the story show somewhat historically what activities occurred on an old farm in the late 1800s. Many of these activities have ceased with time, yet it is well that they be recorded in the annals of old farm life. Included are stories about such things as the ice house, chestnuts and chinquapins, farm buggies, "thrashing", the one-room school and more than 60 ways of life that were common 100 years ago.

The stories woven around Young George and his family were created after interviewing many older citizens who lived in this early period, as well as my own experiences growing up in like circumstances on a farm in Harford County, Maryland.

For our young readers, you may get tired of trying to keep up with the daily activities of Young George, but I bet you'll end up wanting to live a day or so on that old farm.

George Grier
Uniontown, Maryland

Contents

Introduction
1. Enter Young George
3. The Family Buggy
5. The Animal Village
7. Grandpa's Days Were Tough
9. A Farmer and Gettysburg
11. The Dinner Bell
13. Ole Time Christmas
15. Privy—A Country Bathroom
17. The Butter Churn
19. The Plow—Farmer's Friend
21. The Ice House
23. Apple Butter Stirrers
25. The Springhouse
27. The Farm Wagon
29. A Chicken and An Egg
31. Church on Sunday
33. The Baby Chick
35. Things of Nature
37. Waiting for the Mailman
39. The Choo-choo Train
41. Old Country Store
43. Ye Old Serenade
45. Gees and Haws
47. The Harness Shop
49. Saturday Night Baths
53. A Trip to the Mill
57. Chestnuts and Chinquapins
59. A Milk Cow's Dream
62. The Cold Room
63. Cold Backs in the Winter
65. A Fence or Two
67. The Country Blacksmith
69. A Visit from Huckster Sam
71. The New Penknife

73. Feeding Time at the Barn
75. Peddlers, Tramps and the Like
76. Apples Grow on Trees
79. Horses Versus Mules
81. One Potato, Two Potato
83. One Room School
86. Butchering Days
89. Homemade (Lye) Soap
90. A Trip to the Lime Kiln
92. The Big Red Barn
94. The Seeds of Spring
96. The Hay Crop
98. Thrashing Days of Old
103. Heat of the Summer
106. The Farm's Vet
108. Corn Harvest—Fall Must
111. The Tin Lizzie
113. The Horse Trader
114. The Farmer's Bull
115. When the Snows Blew
119. The Country Doctor
121. Playtime on the Farm
123. A Hunting We Will Go
125. The Old Wooden Pump
127. A Mother's Day
129. That White Mule
131. Grandma's Funeral
134. Country Mud Road
136. The Telephone is Born
138. Grandpa Slows Down
139. Young George Looks at the Future
141. The Tractor Versus The Horse
143. Exit Young George
145. List of Illustrations

Introduction

This is the story of Young George Shaffer, born more than 100 years ago on an old family farm in northern Maryland, just south of the Mason-Dixon Line. George was born September 12, 1894 on his grandfather John Shaffer's 90-acre farm in a small white-washed house near the big red barn. George's father and mother, Roger and Mary, had worked on the farm since their marriage in 1887. They were the mainstay for Grandpa and Grandma, Martha, who were approaching their 70s. Young George had two older sisters, Mildred and Helen who were 6 and 4 when he was born. Brother Ralph was born two years later. Farm life was hard at the close of the 1800s. The Shaffers were dairy farmers. They hauled their milk in a horse-drawn wagon. Horses took them to church—up the road to Bittinger's general store or out the valley road to the mill. And they walked to their neighbors. There were no automobiles—no telephones—no radios. When someone got sick, the country doctor came by horse and buggy with his satchel of pills and home remedies.

Young George was about to enter an exciting, but hard life with many adventures and lots of long hours working in the fields and laboring in the barn. He was stepping into a family held together by love, mutual respect, a deep faith in God and gratitude for the blessings bestowed on them as simple farmers—the keepers of the "old ways".

Enter Young George Shaffer

"Before there were hospitals near farming communities, children of farm families were born at home—sometimes under the care of the old country doctor if his horse and buggy could get him to the farm on time. If not, it was up to the members of the family to do the best they could to bring the baby into his new world."

Roger had harnessed and hooked old Bess, the family's favorite driving horse, to the stick wagon and away they went—down the road to Bittner's country store, for there was going to be a brand new baby at the Shaffer house. The only nearby phone was several miles down the road at the store and old Doc Hering was needed post-haste.

When Roger finally got the doctor's wife on the phone, she said the Doc would be right out as soon as she could get word to him. He would have over eight miles to get out to the farmhouse and by horse and buggy that would take at least an hour and a half after he got the word. In the meantime, Roger raced old Bess back to see how Mary was doing. He would get some water on the stove in case the baby came. He sent the two girls over to Grandma Shaffer's house and she came over to lend a hand if the baby came before the doctor arrived. Doc Hering came riding into the farm lane about dark on that September evening.

As he was looking Mary over, he said, "Roger, how about unhooking my horse from the carriage and finding a fork full of hay and some water for the old mare. She's worked harder than I have today."

When Roger came back in from the barn, Doc Hering said, "Roger, you and Mary have a name for the kid? You know I got to fill in a name on the birth record."

Mary was already having those sharp pains and said, "Doc Hering, Roger and I will name him George if you bring us a boy. The girls want a baby brother too."

Midnight came and went, and the doctor was dozing over in the corner of the room on a chair. He had been up since six in the morning with a sick case out Uniontown way. It was nearing one o'clock when Mary hollered, "Doc, it's time." Doc sprung into action and soon found a real live kicking boy in his hands. He severed the cord and handed Young George Shaffer to Grandma. "Here's a grandson for you Martha."

The Family Buggy

"The buggy was a premature 'tin lizzie' in the days when old Dobbin was the only motor. The covered buggy was for all seasons and all roads, and with a strong horse it was possible to hobble through hub-cap high mud during the spring thaws."

Grandma Shaffer wanted to have a buggy to go to church. Before 1886, however, Grandpa had to take her to church or down to Bittinger's store in the spring wagon. The small wagon had good "springy" springs in both the front and rear and a wooden seat for which she had made a pad filled with straw to sit upon. But Grandma had to have a new buggy in case it rained on Sunday. She found forty six dollars in hidden egg money for Grandpa to go buy one from one of the carriage manufacturers in town. When young George came along he became the favorite grandchild. As soon as he was two years of age, Grandpa and Grandma tucked him in the shiny black buggy between them for the trip to Sunday school and their little German Lutheran Church in the valley. He learned to say "bugg-ie" without too much trouble and always looked for a ride on that soft seat behind old Bess who pulled the light buggy with fair ease. Young George's Papa, Roger, had, a few years before, been able to borrow Grandpa's new buggy when he was "acourtin'" Mary. She had lived over the hill a couple of miles, and Roger always tried to borrow the buggy to go see her on Saturday nights if he wasn't too late helping Grandpa with the feeding and milking. He had learned to wash Old Bess down with strong coffee to make her shine, and, of course, he had washed the buggy too.

Farmers got to town in their buggies or wagons for the bare necessities. Note the hitching rail. When there was not enough room at the rail, the horse was left standing in the road. Note the dog sleeping on the buggy seat awaiting the master.

Buggies and wagons line up outside a carriage manufacturer before 1900. The shop was the hub of activity in town, for all farms needed good wagons and buggies. It took about a week to make a buggy.

No doubt this young farmer has not only put on his "Sunday Best" for his date, but he's shined his horse and carriage also.

Roger usually went to sleep in the buggy on the way home from seeing Mary with the reins hanging on the dashboard and around the whip socket. Old Bess would bring him back to the farm stopping at the wagonshed where Roger blew out the lantern hanging on the side of the buggy. Roger then unhooked her and took her into her stall next to the stable door.

Mary always told Roger, "I hope we get a buggy if we get married." They got married a year later in 1887, but no buggy.

Most farms around the Shaffers used the spring wagon (sometimes called the "stick" wagon) for all the light traveling work—going to church, the store, or the mill for a light load of feed. They used it also to haul the milk cans to the neighboring farmers' milk stand.

Its springs made the ride over the dirt roads fairly comfortable, and it was made of light materials and easy for one horse to pull. Then too, on trips to church the kids could squeeze in the back and sit on an old blanket or some straw. In real cold weather Mama made sure the kids carried a heated brick or stone to keep warm.

The old buggy which had cover for both rain and snow was sometimes considered the sign of prosperity—so to speak. Not all families around the valley had one or could afford to pay $25 to $50 for a buggy and also pay for their work wagons, horses and mules.

And so, the two Shaffer families shared in the use of Grandpa's buggy. If it happened to be in use, there was always the spring wagon.

The Animal Village

"Farms were centered about the barn. It housed most of the large farm animals—stored the food that fed them, and the farmer probably spent more time in the farm buildings than in his own house."

Young George Shaffer, from the time he was able to toddle around, usually wandered off to the chicken house or the barn in search of his fun day. It was live animals that caught him up in an excitement that only farm kids knew.

He would tell his mama, "Me go to barn with Papa". And of course there was the understanding that Papa would take the responsibility for the safety of his young son among the cows, horses, calves and pigs.

The Shaffer farm village had many buildings where their farm animals slept or stayed when the winter winds howled unmercifully. Chief among the buildings was the big red barn with the white cupola on its roof.

The barn was built like many in the mid-1800s with chestnut siding and rafters which were pegged and a shingled roof atop. Then there was the the chicken house, wagonshed, with corn cribs on both sides and a pig house—sometimes called a sty.

During the later part of the 1800s Grandpa added an ice house, springhouse, a separate corn crib, carriage building and a half dozen smaller buildings used for calves, sheep and farm implements.

Grandpa and Grandma bought the 90 acre farm in 1857 with the buildings all being on the side of a hill with a warm southern exposure in winter months. The heavy rains drained downhill to a small stream in the valley pasture below the barn.

At the age of two Young George was able to link the noises made by each farm animal. The turkey gobbled—the sheep baa'd—the pig squealed and grunted, the horses whinnied, while the mules brayed.

(cont'd)

Chickens made up a large part of the animal village population.

Young George knew each cow moo and recognized Lucy, the cow, because she had a tinkling cow bell around her neck. He usually heard the roosters crow beginning at dawn as he was climbing out of bed early in the morning.

For his second birthday, Young George's Papa got him a bench-legged brown and white beagle hound which he named Soybean. Soybean was a barker and slept under the warm kitchen stove at night.

In the years before Young George was born in 1894, Grandpa believed he had one of the best farms around. He and his son Roger had gathered around them a team of six good horses, two mules and a herd of 10 or 12 excellent milking cows. They had a chicken house full of white and red laying chickens, a half dozen turkeys (which lived in the trees at night) and a few guinea hens—the noisy "watch dogs".

The 60 acres of tillable land had been rotated, well limed and manured each year to produce good hay, corn, wheat and other crops for the farm animals to eat. The fields of clover and timothy were well set.

The red brick house where Grandpa and Grandma lived was in pretty good shape as was the white tenant house where Papa and his family lived. Both houses would soon be made more comfortable when running water and bathrooms were put in.

There was no doubt the Shaffer families could live forever in their little farm village of cows, horses and other animals without really depending on the outer world, except to sell their milk, butter, eggs and extra farm produce or crops.

Their little farm village fed the Shaffer family—provided most of the joys of farm family living, as well as the opportunity to go to church on Sundays to worship with their neighbors.

And that was true of a good many other farm families in the hills and dales of this Maryland countryside in the days of the "horse and buggy".

Grandpa's Days Were Tough

Sarah Brunst

Young George's Grandpa, John Shaffer, was almost 70 when Young George was born. He had many stories to tell his grandson about farm life in the last half of the 1800s. Young George looked forward to being with Grandpa for he was a warm and kind man, but had a sternness which came from his German upbringing.

Grandpa John Shaffer's time goes well back into the 1800s. It was a time when oxen were used on farms though draft horses were quickly taking over, and the binder and reaper were replacing the cradle and flail.

Grandpa was one of ten children and was born near Hanover in southern Pennsylvania. He married a neighbor, Martha Rhinehart, in 1857.

The members of the Shaffer clan were long-time inhabitants of northern Maryland and southern Pennsylvania. Grandpa's grandparents came to America in the late 1700s—landed in Philadelphia and settled in the southern part of Pennsylvania. As did almost 75 percent of the American population in the 1800s, the Shaffers were farmers, and Grandpa believed this was to be his way of life too.

(cont'd)

He sometimes wondered if his kinfolk also included families who spelled their names Schaffer, Schaeffer, Shaefer or Shafer. He told Martha he reckoned they forgot to spell way back when, and added or subtracted some of the letters.

Grandpa's father lived and farmed on about 60 acres in southern Pennsylvania, not far north of the Mason and Dixon line. His nine brothers and sisters, like Grandpa, were well-schooled in milking cows, hoeing and cutting corn as well as the daily chores familiar to the members of any farm family.

When Grandpa and Grandma Martha Rhinehart were married in 1857, they looked around for a farm they could call their own rather than working as tenant farmers for a neighbor or another family member. Fortunately, Martha's father, Jacob Rhinehart, came to the young couple's aid and loaned them $500 to put down on a 90-acre farm in northern Maryland that had been advertised in the "American Sentinel" newspaper. Then Grandpa was able to borrow $2,000 from a local bank. The Shaffers' new farm had an old bank barn, a wagonshed, a couple of chicken coops and a brick house which they were able to move into without too much work. It was a small two-story house with four bedrooms, a kitchen, dining room and small parlor. Also on the farm was a small frame house that could be used as a tenant house or perhaps used by their children as they grew older.

Grandpa was able to get started on his farming venture with the help of some neighbors and his brothers who would come down from Pennsylvania for a week or two during the harvest. It didn't take Grandpa and Grandma long to get their new farm producing some good crops, and gradually they were able to build up a small herd of holstein cattle. Their first child was born in the first year at their farm. Young George's father, Roger, was the fifth child— born in 1866.

Life on the farm in this era was tough. The telephone had not been even dreamed of, and communication was one of word and mouth between farms. The winters were bitter cold. The roads were but narrow dirt paths and almost impassable each winter and early spring because of the mud and snow. The country stores were few and far between, and many did not carry anything other than bare essentials like leather for a harness, coal oil for lamps and maybe some yard goods to make or patch farm clothing. It was up to the farm family to raise its own chickens, eggs, meat supplies and vegetables. There was only a doctor or two in each town, and a school perhaps on a neighboring farm that could accommodate a dozen students with a volunteer teacher.

Grandpa's family was happy and hard-working. He read the family Bible each night after the evening meal, and was able to quote it chapter and verse. He made sure Grandma put the kids to bed at eight and got them up at four to do their farm chores before breakfast at seven. Typically, none of the children got off the farm to go to town until they were grown and on their own.

Despite the harsh weather, this family was inching along toward having one of the best farming operations in the valley. Roger married in 1887, and the couple decided to stay on the farm with Grandpa and Grandma making the future of the Shaffer farm seem brighter—particularly so upon the birth of Young George in 1894.

A Farmer and Gettysburg

> "A lot of people were affected by the Battle of Gettysburg, including soldiers, doctors and even farmers. As troops scoured the countryside looking for food and clothing, farmers who were paid a visit by soldiers of the Confederate and Union Armies sometimes lost horses and cattle with little or no remuneration."

The John Shaffer family had barely gotten their farming operation started when the Confederate and Union troops were assembling in the Gettysburg area in June and July of 1863 to meet in a battle that would be considered one of the largest of the Civil War.

The soldiers of both armies had been rapidly moving north and were in great need for many things an army needed—food and clothing as well as horses, mules, wagons and feed for the animals. Sometimes a cow or flock of chickens were taken when a group of soldiers came into a farm.

The Shaffer farm was not far from the Gettysburg scene. Even though the Shaffers had a long lane, it did not stop hungry soldiers from coming in from the main road in search of something to eat.

Grandpa Shaffer was wise to what was happening and took his horses into the farm woods of the farm and hid them. He hoped that they would not nicker and give away their hiding place.

Grandma on the other hand, when she saw the hungry and dusty soldiers, cooked and fed them regardless of the time of day. Her hot bread and smoked ham must have satisfied the soldiers, for the Shaffer cows and chickens were not disturbed by three different contingents of soldiers who found their way back to the farm. Many of the Shaffer neighbors lost horses, and wagons, as well as calves and heifers.

The Shaffers dreaded to hear the noise of battle those first three days of July. The guns could be heard clearly as if they were just across the hill.

(cont'd)

During the final weeks of June 1863 Union and Confederate troops funneled from all directions into the countryside of northern Maryland and southern Pennsylvania and gathered provisions from many of the local farmers along the way. The ensuing Battle of Gettysburg claimed over 51,000 lives. Peace would not come for another two years.

The Dinner Bell

"The old dinner bell was the chief, and probably the only, way to communicate between farms if there was an emergency. It served also as a way for the farm wife to call in the men from the fields for their noon meal. Oddly enough, it let the horses and mules know it was time for a drink of water, and some corn if they too had been working by pulling equipment in the fields."

Young George always wanted to yank the rope that was tied to the big black dinner bell which was fastened to the top of the long cedar post just outside the kitchen door. Of course Mama always kept the rope tied high enough on the bell post so that the kids would not ring the bell when they weren't supposed to. She did hold Young George up one day and let him ring the bell for the men who were plowing in the field above the barn.

The old iron bell had a different tone for each farm. Farmers could usually tell whose bell was ringing for the dinner meal or an emergency.

One clear day when Papa was coming in for dinner he said that he could hear dinner bells ringing from about seven nearby farms telling their men it was time to eat. In those cases, the farmer's wife would not have to go out and yell for her men to come eat.

About two months before, Papa heard a farm bell continuously ringing, and he immediately jumped on one of the horses and rode down the road to see why the bell had been ringing so long. As he came closer, he noticed smoke, and when getting to the farm lane, he immediately saw a field fire that seemed to be burning close to his neighbor's farmhouse. In this case, he and several adjoining neighbors worked together beating out the flames before they got to the house or any of the farm buildings.

(cont'd)

Aided by a large wood or coal-fired cookstove, the farm wife could turn out a feast for the hungry men.

The Shaffer's two mules, Sam and Joe, were aware that the dinner bell, when ringing, meant it was time to go to the barn. Consequently Papa could not get those mules to make another round pulling the harrow once Mama had rung the bell. Old Sam and Joe pranced around and refused to go back across the field for another round until they were taken to the barn for a drink of water, their corn and a fork full of hay.

The Shaffer bell had sounded loud and clear over the years. Although it had been used to mark a death or sound the alarm for emergencies, that bell was Mama's way of calling her men to eat.

Modern cooking ware like this was offered in the 1897 Sears Roebuck catalog. This assortment of "kitchen furniture" was priced at $3.50 then.

Ole Time Christmas

> *"Christmases go back centuries, and they each brought a special meaning to all people. For the farm family, the celebration was usually the same—togetherness and maybe one small present with an orange, some hard candy and a blessed meal on Christmas day."*

Young George quickly learned what Christmas was all about—his older sisters made sure of that. He watched them go with Papa to find and cut a Christmas tree up on the hill. It was a cedar tree which they dragged down through the snow and put up for Santa Claus to trim.

They all were put to bed early, but awoke early on Christmas morning to find that the magical person, called Santa, had gotten into the house. Papa said he came down through the chimney, but the girls said it wasn't big enough.

Anyway, all that questioning was forgotten when Young George and his sisters were allowed to go into the parlor on that Christmas morning and there it was. The tree was all decorated with large and small colored balls, make-believe horns, and strings of long white pop corn.

They each found their stocking hanging. Mama helped Young George find his. His hand reached down into that old green stocking and found one big round and cold orange—the first he had ever seen. He reached down a little further and out came a box of hard, red and green candy—the real store-bought kind.

Over near the parlor stove there were three packages—one for Young George and one each for Mildred and Helen. "Open them up," said Papa. "Let's see what Santa brought you."

Mildred got a new red dress—Helen, new black shoes and Young George found in his package a pair of new socks and a tiny pair of "bib overalls"—just like his Papa's. His Mama had made them out of a pair of Papa's old overalls he had worn out and thrown away.

"And now," Papa said. I've got to go down to the barn and see if Santa came to see the cows and horses."

"Do you really think so," Helen asked? And Papa replied, "I don't know, but if he wasn't there, I'll give them an extra fork full of hay. The horses won't be working on Christmas day.

(cont'd)

And now it was Mama's turn. "I've got to work on Christmas dinner, and you girls have to help me. We're having Grandpa and Grandma over for our Christmas dinner. They'll want to see your presents."

Mama had cooked a large rooster for the dinner. She brought up from the cellar jars of string beans, peas, corn and tomatoes. She also got potatoes, carrots and turnips from the sand pile in the cold room. Mildred said, "Young George. We're going to have a real Christmas dinner nice enough for a king."

Of course, Grandpa and Grandma came on time for dinner, but they wanted to see Young George's Christmas presents first. He held them up and said, "See". Grandpa then gave him ten cents, and said, "This is for your bank." And the girls, too, got their ten cents.

The cedar tree was the popular Christmas tree in the 1900 era.

For dinner Grandpa was asked to give the blessing:

"On this Christmas day of 1896, we give thee our thanks. We pray that all little girls and boys have a happy Christmas day. O, Lord, our God. We thank thee for our family and the good dinner we are about ready to eat."

Amen

The Christmas celebration was not over. There came a knock on the door when the snowy darkness had come. "Who could that be?" Mama called. "Go see Mildred."

Lo and behold, there were six people who had on masks. Their horses and sleighs were out front. At first Mildred was scared, and Helen and Young George ran to hide. Papa said to the masked friends, "Come on in and enjoy our home on Christmas night."

Mama had prepared for these guests and maybe more to come. Cookies and cakes were taken out of the large pantry lard can and put on the table with root beer. The coffee had been made.

Mama had known about the visit from the neighbors and was ready in time. "Kris Kringling" celebrations with neighbors was a tradition many farm families eagerly looked forward to during Christmas time.

The Privy
A Country Bathroom

"Most farm families in the late 1800s probably never enjoyed the luxury of an indoor toilet or bathroom. It was to the "outhouse" or "privy" that they went to in all kinds of weather—night and day."

Young George went through his "potty training" until he was two years of age. That consisted of using the old white china pot kept under his small crib-like bed. His Mama, Mary, did not have any trouble with Young George after he was one year old because he would kneel down on the floor and "pee" into the pot. It was too big to fit his "posterior" so his Mama would have to hold her hands under his arms until he finished his "duty".

When Young George reached his second birthday, he was getting inquisitive, and asked his Mama, "Why can't I go to outdoor privy like you, Papa and sisters?" The word "privy" was like any other word a one or two-year-old kid learned to say because the word was used over and over again by the entire family, day in and day out.

From then on, Mildred, being the oldest child of the Shaffer family, got the newest daily chore—that of taking Young George out to the privy behind the house and setting him on the smallest of the two holes in the privy. She then held him by his arms until he was finished.

As curiosity grew, he asked his sister Mildred one day, "Why is one hole small and one hole big?" Mildred replied,"Why Young George, Mama and Papa have to use this privy too, and they are big people." He then pointed to the little half moon in the door , and again Mildred explained that the half moon was for seeing who might be coming to the privy.

During the next year or so, Young George found out the answers to more questions, such as why was the old Sears Roebuck catalogue always in the privy. Sister Mildred again explained that everyone looked at the pictures. Catalogues, like Sears Roebuck, which found their way from the farmhouse to the privy, were like a fairyland for the kids and older members of the family too. The less interesting sheets were torn out and used for toilet paper, like the corn cobs in the box on the floor.

(cont'd)

A "two-holer" was the most popular privy or outhouse accommodation. This "three holer" was no doubt needed by a large family.

Young George always looked for those large black spiders he could smash and kill on the privy's inside wooden walls. He often wondered why the spiders liked living in the privy. When he grew older, he would often boast to one of the neighbor boys that he had a "two-holer" and they only had a "one-holer". The neighbor boys called their privy an "outhouse".

The only time Young George hated to go to the privy was when it was real cold. He would say to Mildred that his rear end was freezing as he sat on the hole. But, of course, if Young George, or any other member of the family got caught short during the night, they lit the old lantern and went to the privy or pulled the old china pot from under the bed. But then, the lady of the Shaffer farmhouse had the job of emptying it outside in the morning.

The Butter Churn

"Putting cream in a glass jar and shaking it from side to side until it comes out as butter was a mystery to even the youngest of farm kids."

At two, Young George could barely turn the handle of his Mama's big wooden butter churn. Yet his sisters made sure that he was well aware that soon he would be old enough to take "his turn" during the buttermaking days at the Shaffer farm.

Grandma had given over the buttermaking responsibilities to Mama and the Shaffer kids. Huckster Sam still looked forward to buying several pounds of their sweet golden butter on his regular Wednesday trips to the farm. The Shaffer butter was always the first butter his Baltimore customers wanted on his weekly excursions to the city.

Every morning Mama went to the springhouse and skimmed off the thick and rich-looking cream from the top of the milk brought up from the barn the night before.

The plunger or stomper butter churn allowed the housewife to stand and move the plunger up and down until she felt the butter "breaking". It held eight to ten gallons.

About three times each week she poured the cream in large stone crocks until there was enough to churn.

Young George would always say to his Mama, "My turn to churn butter." His sister Helen would echo, "Yes it is, Mama." For Helen hated the chore of turning the handle of the butter churn.

The round cylinder churn was popular because it could be cranked easily, and a child could turn the handle too.

(cont'd)

Sometimes butter churning was a long, tiresome and hot job. However, it wasn't long before Papa had weaned away Young George to help with the feeding down at the barn, so Mama and the girls had to do the churning themselves.

Mama always had her brown wooden cylinder churn clean. Before using it she would fill it with water to make sure the cracks were sealed and that it wouldn't leak. One day Mama hoped to be able to buy a "dash" churn—one in which a long handle was used to plunge up and down in an upright barrel, In the summertime she did the butter churning in the springhouse. In the winter the warm kitchen was the scene of the churning job.

Young George always said the first turns of the butter churn sounded like a "bunch of frogs" down in the meadow pond as the thick cream plopped around for 10 to 15 minutes depending on how cold the cream was. In the summer or hot days, Mama would use some ice from the ice house or add cold water to the churn to make sure the particles of butter would "gather" together when it "broke" from cream to butter. Young George would always yell "butter here" when the slow "swishing" sound changed to a "splashing" sound from inside the churn.

Mama raised the lid on the churn to be sure the butter particles had appeared inside, but the churning had to continue until there was a dead thudding and thumping inside the churn—like "thump-ker-thump". Soon all eyes were peering down in the churn to stare at the mounds of golden butter that had gathered together in the buttermilk.

The butter print pressed the farm wife's mark on each pound of butter she sold.

Mama and Papa loved buttermilk to drink, but most of it ended in the pigs slop barrel.

The final butter operation was strictly Mama's. She gathered every lump of butter in the churn and placed it in a wooden bowl. She worked it with her flat wooden paddles with frequent changes of cold water. As soon as she had pushed all the water from the large glob of butter, a sprinkling of salt was put on top. Mama carried the butter to the cellar and reworked it the next day to pull out any remaining moisture.

The Shaffers used a wooden butter print which pressed a decorative design into each mound of butter. They also turned the butter out into long rolls which Huckster Sam could cut to suit his customers. And Mama always kept butter for use in her kitchen.

The Plow—Farmer's Friend

"The plow was the very first thing the farmer had to buy for turning his soil and getting ready to plant his seeds. A blacksmith named John Deere, fortunately, had developed his new steel plow which made plowing a bit easier by the mid-1880's.

Young George had almost turned two years of age and Roger, his papa, was beginning to believe he had a buddy—for now that Young George was walking and running, he wanted to go everywhere his papa went.

This early May day was another plowing day for soon it would be corn planting time. Roger decided he would let Young George walk behind him in a newly plowed furrow with a tin can picking up fishing worms for a fishing trip down to the pond or in Pipe Creek later on. That way he could watch Young George until he grew tired of walking and then his mama could take him back to the house.

Roger had been plowing now for some 15 years. He had just put on a new plow shear, frog and mouldboard on the old wooden beam one-man plow. With his good team of horses and a sharp eye, he watched the soil turning over as the mouldboard flipped over that first clean-cut twelve inch furrow in a straight path across the whole length of the field. This was the objective of farmers 70 to 100 years before him.

John Deere

The Shaffer horses, after they heard Roger's "gidap", looked at each other, bobbed their heads together, and stepped off in unison. This meant their collars tightened together and away they went across the field pulling the plow.

Roger's lead horse, Maude, always responded to the lightest touch

(cont'd)

on her line and at the end of the field she was always thinking ahead and waiting for Roger to touch that line and head back across the field. Most farmers knew their horses and mules. In fact, most knew all there was to know about the "south end of a northbound mule."

Roger kept his eye on Young George and soon saw Mama leading him back to the house, tin can and all.

Roger was recognized by local farmers as one of their best in the area. He knew, for instance, that he could finish plowing two to three acres a day, and in walking behind that bouncing 100-pound plow, that meant about 16 miles of walking in that soft, fresh dirt.

He would be ready for bed at nightfall. Grandpa Shaffer had almost given up walking behind a heavy plow. He, however, walked behind the spring-tooth harrow used to break up the plowed furrows—then rode a heavy homemade wooden drag which finished breaking up most of the large clods of dirt which needed to be done before planting corn.

Fortunately, Roger had finished at least half of his plowing the previous fall after corn harvest had been finished. Fall plowing not only buried the weeds and insect eggs, but he knew that fall plowing aerated the soil over the winter months and held the moisture needed for spring crops.

A Rhyme of the Cornfield

Up at early morn
a-plowin' out corn
in the ten acre lot.

I foller the row,
whistlin' as I go—
goodness, ain't it hot!

Sun two hours high—
Suds, but I'm dry!
Guess'll go'n git a drink.

Been't the house most'n hour
An' now't's goin to shower.
Have to stop, I kinder think.

An hour's a nooin' past,
back to work at last—
didn't rain, after all.

Plowed five rows more;
Now't's half past four—
wish the hired girl'd call.

Down goes the sun;
only ten rows done,
not two hours' stiddy work.

D'ye reely want to know
why I've been s'awful slow?
'Taint because I'm a shirk.

I kinder hate ter tell,
but I guess I might as well—
no, it ain't any hoax.

Won't wonder I worked slow,
I guess, when you know—
she's a-vis'tin' our folks.

The Ice House

"Long before the ice man cometh, many farmers relied upon a pond or stream from which they cut ice and hauled it to their underground ice house—thus assuring ice for the farm family and church socials in the warmer months of the year."

When Grandpa John Shaffer bought his farm in the northern Maryland hills in 1859, he, of course, looked over the land and farm buildings before he even looked at the farmhouse. At that time he told his young bride, Martha, "I like the lay of this land except that little corner of land down by the woods. Looks to me like it is too wet to plow or farm, and it won't grow good trees either."

For years after, Grandpa Shaffer didn't plow or farm that wet area of land. He just farmed around it. One day after his youngest son, Roger, got married and moved into his white tenant house with Mary, his bride, Grandpa said, "Roger, I'm going to borrow a scoop somewhere. With the horses I believe we can scoop out a pond and raise some fish and some ice." Roger questioned, "How do you raise ice?"

"Well, you and I are going to build that pond and an ice house up here near the farm buildings. Each winter when it gets really cold, we'll cut that ice and fill the ice house, and have ice cream in the summer," said Grandpa.

The ice house was usually underground. Ice would keep most of the hot summer months because the dirt or stone walls was an insulation.

When not busy with the milking and harvest work, Grandpa and Roger found a scoop and with their horses started scooping out the dirt and "muddy" muck from that small wet area next to the woods.

Soon those little springs that had made the area wet began running into the new pond. As it turned out the Shaffers had a pond about three feet deep and about one-half acre in area. Grandpa told some neighbor kids to go fishing in Pipe Creek and catch some fish for his new pond.

After the spring planting season the following year, Grandpa had Roger scooping out an area next to the wagon shed, hoping that he would not hit rock before he had a hole dug about ten feet deep and ten feet wide. During the winter, Grandpa and he had cut several oak logs to put around the dirt walls of the new ice house. "When ice is

(cont'd)

hauled from the pond, these walls will be covered with fodder," Grandpa said. "Roger, you and John Bankert now have to put a roof on these walls. And don't forget a trap door large enough to slide large blocks of ice down into the ice house, and in the summer, a place to use a ladder when we need it."

And so in the winter of 1889, the Shaffer family started filling their new ice house. It was after the Thanksgiving butchering and cold enough for the ice to freeze almost 12 inches thick on the pond. Old Jake Yingling, a neighbor across the hill, was asked to help in the first ice harvest. He had helped other farmers for many years to cut ice for their ice houses. Old Jake started by cutting a large hole in the ice in the center of the pond with an axe. He then showed Grandpa how to use a small short crosscut saw to make two, 24-inch wide cuts some 19 or 20 feet long. These could be pushed out of the water with large pike poles. Once out of the water, the long pieces were cut into smaller 24-inch blocks and pulled with tongs to the bobsled, loaded, and hauled up to the ice house. If there was no snow on the ground, the large wagon would be used to haul the ice. Each piece of ice was slid on a large board down to the dirt floor which was covered with saw dust. As the pieces were laid out on the saw dust floor at the bottom of the ice house, they were covered with more saw dust or even oak leaves. The very top layer of ice was covered with saw dust, fodder or straw. Then the door was closed until pieces of ice were needed.

Grandpa said to Martha that last evening of the ice harvest, "Martha, I want you to plan on ice cream this summer. And you'll have ice to keep your butter and eggs cool until Huckster Sam comes. We can even have a cake of ice on hot summer days to cool our milk in the springhouse."

The Shaffer families were happy. Not all farms had ice houses. And they could now fish in the pond or skate on the ice in the winter.

An interior view of the ice house with stone walls shows a ladder leading down to a depth of about ten feet.

the Apple Butter Stirrers

"To stir apple butter in the old copper kettle and to smell the cooking apples and wood smoke was an all-day experience for all members of the family. Indeed, it provided another source of good farm food - food for each farm family who had a small apple orchard or bought apples from a neighbor."

Apple butter was made in a large copper kettle and needed constant stirring to keep from burning and sticking to the sides.

Usually on the first crisp fall October day, all eyes in the Shaffer family turned to getting ready to make apple butter. It took a day or so to get the dried apple wood ready, the copper kettle out of the shed and the apples pared and cut up to be cooked the next day.

It was not uncommon to smell the sweet-burning apple or hickory wood smoke on cool October days coming from the farms who had also decided it was time to make apple butter.

Grandpa Shaffer and his wife, Martha, started getting apples from their small orchard in 1882. They went to a farm sale and bought an old copper kettle with several scrapers, stirrers and gallon crocks for preserving their applebutter.

For the first year of apple butter making, Grandpa depended on family members and a neighbor or two to help, but as the Shaffer family grew it became an annual family affair. Apple butter day was held soon after corn cutting. Roger and Mary, following their marriage, took over most of the organizing of the yearly apple butter event and Young George and his sisters in the early 1900s were accepted as good substitutes for Grandpa and Grandma.

Young George's first job when he was two years of age was to help his Papa build the apple butter fire at five o'clock in the morning. Fact is, he scarcely slept when his Papa said, "Young George your job will be to help your Papa get the old apple wood from the wood shed and stack it near where we can put it on the fire under the kettle tomorrow morning."

(cont'd)

The apples had to be gathered from the ground or picked from the trees and carried to the cellar where they would be pared and cut up to go into the kettle.

A neighbor, Mrs. Bixler, worked with Grandma and Mama for most of the day getting the apples ready to put in the kettle for cooking which began at five in the morning.

It was always understood that Grandpa Shaffer was to be the first "stirrer"—he had had the most practice in the years before. It was Grandpa who said to those gathered at the early morning ceremony that "the stirrer had to push then pull the long wooden stirrer on a figure eight path" through the cooking apples to prevent them from sticking to the side of the kettle as they cooked all day long. As the wood was put under the kettle, Grandpa warned his workers not to have red hot coals touch the bottom of the kettle lest it burn a hole in the bottom of the kettle.

The apple stirrers were usually made from either apple or sassafras wood. Traditional thinking had it that anything touching apples had to be made of wood, or the flavor would be spoiled.

Grandma Shaffer decided what went in that kettle besides apples, for it was her recipe that always brought the Pennsylvania relatives for some apple butter cooked by the Shaffers. Among items gotten from Bittingers Store was plenty of sugar and cinnamon which made the dark apple butter a tasty part of any daily dinner or supper meal at the Shaffer Farm.

The whole family took turns in pushing and pulling the long wooden stirrer back and forth through the apples as they cooked. The kettle had been put on the fire at five in the morning and was still cooking at two in the afternoon. Grandma was usually the official taster as it neared its final cooking stage. The important part she said," was not to let the apples stick to the side of the kettle and burn, or the apple butter would be ruined."

Young George took his turn at stirring, but it was short-lived for the smoke from the wood fire under the kettle blew into his eyes and he said, "I'm too little to stir, Papa, your turn."

Dipping out the cooked apple butter from the kettle took another hour. Most of it was put in gallon crocks and put down in the cellar of Grandpa's house. There was enough to last two families until next year, as well as, to give a few gallons to the pastor, some visitor friends and those who helped. Sometimes Mama would sell a pot for one dollar. Papa scraped and cleaned the old copper kettle, scrapers and stirrers then stored them in one of the sheds for next year's apple butter day.

the Springhouse
A Farm Refrigerator

The springhouse was always located downhill from the spring which furnished the water to cool the milk. It was also cool enough to keep the butter, cream and eggs.

"Most wise farmers, when looking to purchase a farm a century or so back, looked to see whether there was a natural spring, the waters of which were capable of being diverted through a springhouse, and on out into a meadow where the cows and horses could drink as they grazed.

The Shaffer farm was blessed from the beginning with a large, natural spring that surfaced in a round pool of water under a massive oak tree near the brick farm house. Papa always held Young George as he bent down to see how cold the spring water was. He would say, "Papa. Water cold."

Grandpa Shaffer, when he first purchased the farm shortly before the Civil War, gathered enough field stone to erect a ten-foot building next to his "spring tree". He allowed the water from the spring to run through his newly erected springhouse in a trough about three feet wide and with three levels of water—24 inches, 15 and 6. His milk cans would be put in the 24 inch section while Grandma used the shallow sections for cooling her butter and other perishable foods.

There was a tin dipper hanging on the side of the springhouse, and was used by everyone to "wet their whistles"

(cont'd)

on hot summer days. With the springhouse door closed, it was always cool, and in the summer Grandma and Young George's Mama kept their butter and eggs inside awaiting Huckster Sam.

As the water passed through the springhouse trough, it ran out into a small ditch in the pasture, but soon Grandpa had constructed a large stone trough to catch some of the overflow where the horses and cattle could drink. From this point, the overflow of water followed a small stream through the pasture.

Water was carried from the spring to the houses, and it was one of Young George's chores to carry water to the chickens, calves and pigs. And, of course, during the hot days of summer, he had to carry a bucket of water to the men in the fields.

Young George also had to whitewash the inside stone walls of the springhouse each spring.

A channel of cool, spring water ran thru the trough in the springhouse where milk, eggs and butter were kept from spoiling, and the milk was cooled.

The Farm Wagon

A lot of wagons and buggies were bought at the old country sale.

"Farm families for 250 years after the settlement of America had only the wagon to travel from farm to farm or community to community. Its only motor was the horse or mule, and the objective of each wagon maker was to make the wagon easier for the animals to pull.

Grandpa, following his marriage in 1857, had only the spring (stick) wagon to take Martha, his wife, to the church. Once they had bought their farm, Grandpa's first purchase at a farm sale was a heavy wagon "gear" which was capable of holding a hay carriage or rectangular body in which to haul corn or wood. Dependent upon the load it was usually pulled by two or four horses guided by check lines.

When Young George came along some 37 years later and was about three years old, he would say, "Papa, can I ride in the big wagon?" Papa would let him stand up in the wagon and look over the sides as they drove to the woods for a load of wood. Sometimes he would let him sit beside him on the large wooden seat where he could look down on the horses as they pulled the wagon.

(cont'd)

This large wagon is filled with feed. Note the right wheel horse is being mounted. The driver will control the team from there.

27

In 1897 this was Sears, Roebuck and Company's finest farm wagon...with wheels which are well ironed and boiled in hot oil. Hubs are best oak and black birch. Spokes are strictly select. Felloes (rims) finest white oak. Axles select young hickory. Gear select white oak. Boxes are made of clear yellow poplar. Bottom boxes made of long leaf yellow pine. Paint is strictly pure and carefully applied by brush and positively no dipping of any kind." The "gear" could be purchased without a box.

There were times when Grandpa and Papa took the wagon bed off the gear and hauled logs up to 20 feet long from down in the woods. The logs extended from the front to the rear axle beams which were connected together by a "pole" or a "reach".

Then in harvest season, Papa would lift the hay carriage onto the wagon gear to haul hay into the barn or sheaves of wheat to the barn to await the thresherman.

Wagon makers hired blacksmiths, carpenters, trimmers and painters. Most wagon makers specialized in farm wagons, including the well known "spring wagon". Many also had a flourishing buggy business.

The two-horse team gets the manure spreader to the field, but the hardest job on the farm was loading the spreader with manure from the cow and horse stables.

The most used farm wagon for farm chores was the "spring wagon" which could haul nearly one-half ton with ease, It sold for about $80 and had a spring seat up front and tailgate. It also was fairly comfortable as one horse pulled it along to the railroad or milk stand each morning with the day's milk.

28

A Chicken and An Egg

"Where there is a chicken there is usually an egg. Each was the part of the life of Young George. Often the farm mortgage had to paid with money from the sale of eggs to the local huckster. And the crowing roosters were also counted on to serve as alarm clocks each morning before dawn."

Young George's first words included "Ma-Ma" and "Pa-Pa". He also learned to say "chick-chick" because it was easy to say for a six-month old child. It was easy when his sisters took him to the chicken house as they gathered eggs that had been layed that day.

Almost every afternoon Young George cried to go out to gather eggs from the "chick'chicks" with his sister Mildred. And most of the time Mildred would gather him up in her arms with the old galvanized egg bucket and away they went out among the clucking and squawking chickens to gather the day's eggs.

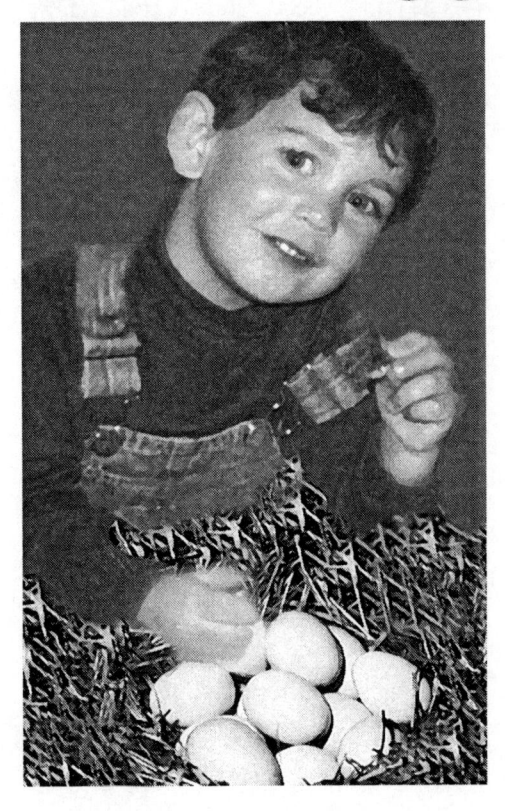

By the time Young George turned four years old he had taken over the job of feeding the chickens by scattering shelled corn or wheat over the chicken yard every morning. Most of the chickens on the Shaffer farm were expected to lay 60 to 100 eggs each year. There were Plymouth Rock, Rhode Island Red chickens as well as two old Bantam hens fighting for the corn that Young George was tossing from his bucket. He liked most the red combs atop the heads of the hens and roosters. He had one favorite chicken he was able to feed from his hand. He told Mama, "Chicken Little lay egg today. I see her on nest."

(cont'd)

During the day the chickens, as on most farms, had free run of the farm. They would scratch here and there for seeds and insects. None dared go far into the field next to the house because they had learned the fear of being swooped down upon by the red-shouldered hawk that normally sat in a tree down in the meadow. The chickens had already seen that hawk carry off a terrified young chicken in its sharp claws.

One day Young George was gathering eggs and had put his hand in a chicken nest, and instead of an egg, he felt a cold moving thing. He stretched his neck and looked in and saw a big black snake with an egg in his mouth. He called, "Papa, come here. Snake in hen's nest." Papa on seeing the critter, grabbed it by the neck. He carried it out to the woods after the snake had twisted around Papa's arm. Letting it loose, Papa told Young George, "Never kill a blacksnake. It keeps the mice and rats away.

At night Young George's job was to see that all the chickens were inside the chicken yard and fence. Grandpa had built the fence to protect his chickens from the foxes and raccoons. Usually the chickens went inside the chicken house and flew up onto the roosts before Young George closed the door. In the morning it was his job to let them out.

That very same year one large grey Plymouth Rock rooster, with its large red comb, took over as chief of the flock. He flew into Young George as he went to feed the chickens—feet first—and his sharp spurs cut Young George's legs. He had heard of mad roosters. Johnnie Yingling told him that they once had a mad turkey gobbler, and his father had to shoot it. Papa also got flogged by the rooster and he said, "Young George, that rooster's gonna either be on our supper table or in Huckster Sam's wagon."

Mama Shaffer took Young George's egg basket each afternoon and carefully washed the brown and white eggs, putting them in the egg crate that Huckster Sam provided farmers to keep their eggs from breaking. On his Wednesday trip to the farm, Sam hoped the Shaffers would have eight to ten dozen eggs as well as their butter for him to buy for his Baltimore customers.

Also going with Huckster Sam sometimes were chickens that were getting too old to lay a lot of eggs.

When Young George started to school he hoped that his little brother Ralph would be feeding the chickens. He then would be taking over the barn feeding chores.

Church on Sunday

"After the milking and the feeding chores were finished early on Sunday mornings, most farm families put on their Sunday best clothes and went off to church. They either walked, rode on a horse, or went by buggy or wagon. It was a day of long sermons—something kids deplored as they longed to get back to the farm. It was not unusual for the pastor and his wife to be invited back with a farm family for a fried chicken dinner, then settle back in the parlor to listen to some music, if the family had a pump organ or piano."

A 19th Century church was heated by several pot belly stoves and lighted by hanging kerosene lamps at night.

The Shaffer family always headed off to church earlier in order to attend Sunday school which was before the regular church services. There were no questions asked about not going either, for Grandpa had made church-going the standard for all his children. He expected their children would be brought up with the same expectations.

The small Sunday school classes were held in each corner of the church. It seemed the grandpas and grandmas were together in one corner; the mamas and papas in another and the kids who were old enough to go to school were in the far corner. In his class, they played little games and also looked at pictures of Jesus. In the summer his Sunday school teacher, Mrs. Lippy, gathered them together under an old sycamore tree outside the church where it was cool. Young George liked that because he could see Mr. Bixler's cows wading in the stream below the church.

Later, when church services started, Young George wondered why he had to sit with Papa and Grandpa on one side (left) of the church. He was four years old now, and he supposed he was a man. Mildred and Helen sat with Mama and Grandma on the right side, and he noticed that little Ralph was sitting on Mama's lap as she listened to the pastor. Young George also noticed they sang the hymns together and bowed their heads when the pastor was saying a prayer. It seemed to Young George that the pastor would never stop talking so he could raise his head and look around.   (cont'd)

Grandpa was a Lutheran because his father and his family had been German Lutherans when he came to America from Leutershausen, Germany in the late 1700s. Young George at four years of age did not understand what a Lutheran was, so he assumed he was a Lutheran too, just like his Papa and Mama.

Young George continued looking around the church while the pastor was preaching. He noticed the seats of the church were divided down the center and that he came in a door (narthex) on his side. The door on the other side where his Mama and Grandma entered went to the seats on their side of the church. He saw coal oil lamps hanging from the wall which could be lit at night. There was a potbelly stove on his side and one on the side where Mama was sitting. They looked just like the ones down at Mr. Bittinger's store. He liked the colored glass in the big window in back of the pastor. He could see through all the windows on the side of the church. Later he asked Mama, "Can we get some pretty red windows like at the church?" And Mama said, "Young George, that glass costs too much money. You find it only in churches."

Young George was glad when church was over. It seemed like the pastor would never stop talking about things he couldn't understand. When he did stop preaching, he had another long prayer. He would be glad to get home on the farm so he could put on his work pants and play down at the barn before milking.

Once in awhile Papa would turn the spring wagon over to Mama so he and Young George could walk home from church. Young George liked that because he would walk past some of the neighbor boys' and girls' farms. He liked to jump over two streams which crossed the old dirt road. There were no bridges. The Fridinger girls who had pretty dresses soon had them messed up crossing those streams as they walked ahead with Young George. He wondered whether their Mama would spank them for getting water and mud on those pretty dresses. Papa would always stop by a neighbor's house and talk farming as they walked home.

Mama had invited the pastor to come for dinner along with Grandpa and Grandma. Papa and Young George got home just in time to greet the pastor and his wife. There was another long grace before they sat down at the table to eat Mama's fried chicken. Young George was not at all happy when Papa said, "Let's move into the parlor room. Perhaps we can sing a little bit."

When Papa said, "Well, it time to go milk," that meant that the pastor and his wife would be leaving and Young George could finally get his old clothes on.

The Baby Chick

The old commercial type incubator was a source of enjoyment for farm kids who could peer inside to see the chicks hatch.

"Spring on the farm always meant nests full of "setting" hens. In each there would soon be peep-peep sounds of the baby chick as it cracked open its egg and looked for a warm place under its mother's wing. The other "peeps" also gathered there as they freed themselves from their shells, and soon they would be taken for their first walk looking for food."

Young George's mother always let a few of her old chicken hens sit on all the eggs she layed. One of Young George's unassigned duties was to find where those "setting" hens were found. While most layed their eggs in the wooden boxes filled with straw in the chicken house, their daily egg was carried to the house in the egg pail. Other old hens hid their nests in the wagon shed, barn or other outbuildings.

It was soon to be Young George's chore to find each chicken's hidden nest and report at the dinner or supper table where he found the nest and when the eggs were beginning to hatch. At the breakfast table on one cool spring morning, Young George announced, "White chicken hatch eggs. I hear a peep-peep."

(cont'd)

Then the next morning he said, "Yellow chicks in white chicken's nest, and Mama let me throw away broken egg shells where baby chicks came out."

It wasn't long before the mother hen had her 10 or 12 chicks scratching on the ground for small insects or seeds for their meal. Young George also spread a little fine cracked corn for them to eat.

Mama Shaffer always supplemented chicks from her "setting hens" with 50 Rhode Island Red chicks that she bought by mail order. The peeping chicks came in a box with small round air holes and dropped off by the mailman at Bittinger's Store.

It was also Young George's job to help get the small white brooder room in the chicken house clean and ready for the new chicks. Papa would light up the small coal brooder stove to keep the chicks warm when they arrived.

Young George soon learned how to put feed in their small feed trough and water in their quart jar water fountains. This was just a new job added to his "big chicken" feeding job each day.

In the days before the brooder, flocks of chickens were raised by the "setting hen" (called broody hens) usually in nests that were hidden or stolen.

34

Things of Nature

"To some extent all kids are caught up in the mysteries that nature provides—whether it be a baby bird on the nest, crawling snakes or worms, or tadpoles turning to frogs. On the old farm, children had a rare opportunity to explore and understand some of the mysteries that were seemingly endless."

Once Young George Shaffer "got his wings", so to speak, his two-year-old inquisitiveness made the days on the farm most interesting. His sisters, his Mama and Papa, and Grandpa and Grandma had to find answers to the multitude of questions he asked. Some of the answers did not come easy.

One of the first things Young George noticed down in the barn were the small bluish-black birds flying in and out of the barnyard. They had pink breasts and a fork-like tail. His first question to his Papa was, "See bird on nest?" Papa answered him by saying, "Those are barn swallows. They eat bugs and take some of them to feed their baby swallows up in that nest on the side of the floor beams."

From that day on, Young George had a love for the twittering song of the barn swallow with the fork on his tail. He looked for them to come back each spring to build their nests on the side of the rafters and push their babies out of the nest when they were ready to fly.

When it came to other birds, Grandpa and Young George were in the woodshed one morning when Grandpa called to Papa, "Look down in the meadow in the old dead chestnut tree. There's a bald eagle with a white head. I bet he has his eye on Grandma's chickens. I better get my gun in case he flies up this way to scoop up a chicken." From that summer day on, Young George knew the difference between the bald eagle and a redtail hawk that also liked to steal chickens. He knew the eerie scream of the hawk down in the woods as he minded his own nest.

One of the strangest sounds Young George had to ask his sisters about was a buzzing sound coming from the trees in the late summer. He learned that the noise was from a locust, and on the side of a tree Papa showed him the brownish shell the locust had broken out of after it had crawled from its sleeping place in the ground. Soon he caught a locust singing on the side of a fence post. That was when he realized its scratchy song came from its tail. The tighter he held the locust, the more it buzzed and squirmed to get loose.

At night during the late summer months, Young George got to know another sound coming from the woods and the old maple tree in the yard. Papa told him the noises were being made by katydids—a light green grasshopper-like flying insect which makes its noise from its wings. The thousands of katydids in the trees, and the crickets in the grass made the sounds of the summer nights a thing of beauty for Young George. He soon learned the katydid sounds meant that summer was coming to an end.

(cont'd)

Back in the early spring, Papa told Mama one day, "The new frogs have started their peepy croaking along the stream in the meadow. It's time to start planting our potatoes." Each year thereafter Young George listened for the "peep-peep" of hundreds of the baby spring frogs.

It was in the springtime that sister Mildred also took Young George for walks through the woods to see the wild flowers while being serenaded by a resident mocking bird. She showed him the purple violets, the yellow dog-toothed violets, jacks-in-the-pulpit, wild geranium, May apples that looked like tiny umbrellas and a blood root flower. "See here," Mildred said. "Break this white blood root and its orange blood runs down on your hand."

Going back home from the woods, they saw what looked like a red dog. Mildred called to Young George, "See that red fox with its bushy tail? I'll bet it's headed up to the chicken house to steal one of Grandma's chickens." Young George said, "I tell Grandpa. He shoot fox."

There were always questions from Young George. "How do fishing worms make holes in the dirt with no teeth or feet?" Then came questions about the bluebird nesting in the fence post. "Who made hole in post for bird? And what made a firefly light up when it got dark?"

Young George went fishing down at the pond with his Papa one day, and there he saw squirming little black "bug-like things" swimming at the edge of the shoreline. Papa said, "Young George, they're tadpoles. Soon they'll grow legs and will be little frogs in three or four months. A frog sits on the bank all day and night and eats the insects they catch. In the wintertime frogs go down into the mud and bury themselves until the weather and water get warm."

Just as important to Young George was watching a cow having a baby calf or a baby chick breaking open an egg to crawl out and find its mother hen to sleep under her wing. Of course, Young George had questions as the calf was being born. Papa managed to be the explainer of what was happening, and told him that in a few minutes the calf would be trying to get her first meal by sucking milk from his mama cow.

Grandma was the instructor on questions about the seed she planted, and how the new plant was able to pop up through the dirt. He watched the corn stalk grow, and the ear of corn grow and make corn silk. He watched the wheat seed being planted. Then in the summer he saw the wheat being thrashed, and the bags of wheat seed coming out of the thresher's hopper. As Young George got near school age, Mama told Papa, "Boy, that kid has learned in five years things I never thought of as a youngster. I hope he does well in school and can tell that teacher a few things about frogs, calves being born and barn swallows catching their meal in the air."

Waiting for the Mailman

The first mail wagons were used in 1899 to start the rural free delivery routes. The wagons delivered mail to key locations and mail carriers took it to individual farms.

"Rural Postal stations (fourth class post offices) located in country stores for the most part, required farmers to pick up their mail. At the country stores tobacco juice was spit and tall tales told—a good bit of which ended around 1900 when a system of rural free letter carriers was started to get the mail to the farmer's door."

Before young George started to school it was his job to walk out the Shaffer's dusty long lane and wait for Mr. Garber, the mailman. Most of the time he could hear him coming up the hill singing as he rode his horse or in his small stick wagon with his sack of mail.

If Young George missed Mr. Garber he would find the mail in an old piece of stove pipe that Grandpa had nailed to a post at the end of his lane as his mailbox. Some farmers used tin cans, cigar boxes or glass jars for the mailman to leave their mail.

When Young George did catch Mr. Garber in time, they always struck up a conversation about the mail and Mr. Garber, who was a jolly sort of fella with a long white beard would say, "Young George, I bet some day you will be a mailman."

Mr. Garber would tell him about the "new RFD Post Office on Wheels"

(cont'd)

and the 26 rural mail carriers like himself. He told him also how he picked up the mail at Bachman's at 10:40 in the morning for delivery on his "C" route. Young George said, "Mr. Garber, I hope I can see that postal wagon some day," to which he replied, "Tell your Papa to ride down to the Mill and maybe the wagon "postal man" will let you climb up in it and see how he stacks the mail for all stations."

The mail for the Shaffer families was never much more than a letter or two from an aunt or uncle. Sometimes Mr. Garber would have a spool of thread for Mama or medicine for Grandma that had been ordered from town. Mr. Garber always left Young George with a merry wave of his hand saying, "I've gotta go—got 18 miles to travel today, and I only have one fresh horse.

"Neither snow nor rain nor dint of night shall keep these mail carriers from their appointed rounds."

Young George liked to look at the stamps on the letters. They were usually pink—marked "two cents" and had a picture of George Washington on it.

Pictured is one of the original mail wagons introduced in 1899 with the advent of Rural Free Delivery (RFD) system created by the Westminster, Maryland post office—the first of such service in the nation. This mail wagon is part of the permanent collection of the Carroll County Farm Museum in Westminster.

The Choo-Choo Train

By the time 1900 rolled around, the steam locomotive had developed into a reliable way to bring the city and country together.

"Most small towns came about in the late 18th or early 19 centuries. For the most part, they served the agricultural people who surrounded the town. Farmers came to town in their wagons and buggies when the necessities of life and the farm required them to do so."

The Shaffer family, as many other farm families, were over an hour's buggy ride from a town. Their trips were done in the daylight hours in their wagon or buggy. To travel at night with only a dimly-lit lantern to guide their horse along some of the narrow dirt roads was not always a safe journey.

For a farmer, the trip was usually to pick up some harness, parts for his wagons or barn equipment. and items not always available at country stores like Bittingers. The rest of the family mostly "saved up" once a year to go to town for yard goods, Sunday shoes and perhaps "lacey" undergarments.

Young George, being Grandpa and Papa's "pie in the sky" boy, went to town whenever he could talk either one of them to take him along. He was three years old when Grandpa took him on his first trip to the town's harness maker.

(cont'd)

This is a typical town of 1900 showing horses, wagons, storefronts and unpaved streets.

The hardware store was a gathering place for farmers who could walk next door to the implement store and find a piece of farm equipment they might need.

They loaded into the spring wagon, and on the way Grandpa said, "Young George, I want to show you your first real train. One should be coming into the train station while we are in town."

While they were at the harness shop, Young George thought he heard a train whistle and he told Grandpa that the "choo-choo was coming". Grandpa hurried and got down to the station in time to see the train coming up the track to the station. Grandpa made sure after the train had stopped to take Young George ahead to the locomotive to talk to the engineer and the fireman. In fact, the fireman took him in his arms up onto the firedeck, and showed Young George where he threw the coal into the fire box. The engineer let him ring the train's bell just as they were about to depart.

That train was the highlight of Young George's trip. Grandpa made sure he stopped at the ice cream store where he bought Young George his first plate of chocolate ice cream. After a trip to the hardware store for some nails , Grandpa stopped at the drug store for some of Grandma's medicines. At both places, Grandpa talked to some farmers about their crops. Going up the main street, Young George pointed to all the tall buildings. There were horses and carriages tied to hitching posts in front along the edge of the dirt street. He saw some men dressed in black clothes coming out of one of the buildings. Grandpa said they were the bankers and that they dressed in business suits every day.

Grandpa showed him where he bought his buggy at the carriage manufacturing plant. He went past the courthouse where he once stopped to see the county commissioners about his road.

Grandpa finally said, "Young George, we'd better get going for it will be milking time by the time we get back to the farm. Young George said, "Grandpa, I like to come to town. There are so may things to see. Can we come again?"

The Old Country Store

The country store was a grocery, hardware, harness and dry goods store under one roof.

"Farm families scarcely needed to go to the store in by-gone days. For most families, food needs were provided by the farm itself. However, the country store was a news source of the goings-on in the community and was also vital for items such as coal oil for their lamps, sugar, spices, coffee or gum boots."

Mr. Sam Bittinger and his wife ran the store down the road three miles from the Shaffer farm. It wasn't far from the Pennsylvania border and on the main road in the valley. The store wasn't anything special. Originally it was a two story house, and the Bittingers added a front porch just after they bought it in the 1870s for things such as coal oil barrels.

There were a couple of worn out benches on the porch where on warm summer evenings farmers would sit and brag about their crops and relate the news of the day—most of which would be hearsay. They could buy a few crackers and cheese for five cents.

The inside of the Bittinger store was jammed with all kinds of stuff, most anything a farmer needed—harness, horse collars, sleigh bells and straps of leather used to repair harness for horses and mules. Then there were shelves full of coal oil (kerosene) lamps, lanterns and lamp globes. Another side of the store was filled with yard goods—ginghams, cotton prints, spools of cotton and pretty white dishes for the farmer wives. There was a section for shoes and slabs of leather for farmers who made their own shoes. You could find on the floor in each corner buckets, cans, brooms, shovels, saws and axes.

There was always a wheel of cheese on the Bittinger counter, as well as the potbelly stove with its long black pipe that went straight up through the ceiling to the roof above. In the winter, the benches came in and seemed to be always filled. Sam provided a tin bucket for those farmers who spit tobacco juice.

(cont'd)

A checker board and dominos sat nearby on a small barrel.

Near the front door the shelves held many things the farmer's wife needed such as spices, tea, coffee and salt. There was a barrel of sugar and two barrels of molasses standing on the floor. Occupying at least six feet of the large counter was a glass case that kept "sticky fingers" from picking up chocolate drops and other penny candy. This was the most impressive thing in the store for a five-year-old kid. From the nose and finger prints on the outside of the glass case, it was evident that neighboring kids had an occasional penny to spend on their favorite gum drop or "chewy gum". And most children probably had trouble making up their minds over which piece of candy they wanted.

Grandpa Shaffer was around when Sam started the store so he knew Grandpa and his sons and daughters. He knew Roger and Mary and soon began recognizing Young George, his sisters Mildred and Helen. He soon took to calling them by their first names as they too liked to gaze down on the candy inside the large glass candy case.

It was not unusual for Young George to have to walk to the country store for his mother. He would ask for a gallon of "Lassy" from the fly-covered molasses barrel, and a can of coal oil for her lamps. Sometimes he had a penny or two left over from the quarter his mother sent along to pay for the purchases. There is no doubt that Young George's nose print was one of many on the glass candy case.

The country store was known for its checkerboard and dominos.

The Bittingers got most of their supplies through some of the local hucksters, including Huckster Sam. These hucksters brought the items ordered by the Bittingers from Baltimore on their return trip where they had been selling their butter and eggs gathered from local farmers. On occasion, the Bittingers also took payment from local farmers by trading eggs and butter for some of their farm needs

Two things happened near the turn of the century which made the store even more useful to the local farm neighborhood. Sam Bittinger, being on a main road got one of the first telephones in the valley. This telephone came just in time for Roger to use for calling the doctor to deliver Young George and his younger brother into the world. In the early part of the 1900s, Sam Bittinger was talking about adding a gasoline pump in front of the store. After all, it would be but a few short years before the "Tin Lizzies" would be riding out into the valley from town and need gasoline.

Ye Ole Serenade

"A young couple getting married could almost expect to receive a special welcome back to the farm by their neighbors. The welcome was in the form of the noisiest and most jubilant banging of pots and pans and other noisemakers available to both young and old."

Young George went to his first country serenade when he was about five years old. The entire Shaffer family wagoned over to the Bitzel farm to serenade Mary Bitzel and her newly acquired husband, Sam. It seemed like the whole countryside was headed to the Bitzels that evening. They brought along all kinds of noisemakers that could be gathered up from around their farms to wish the young couple a happy marriage.

As usual, Young George was all eyes and wanted to see what was about to happen. When they arrived, the bride and groom were nowhere to be seen, however, Mr. and Mrs. Bitzel were inviting their neighbors and friends to gather around the front porch to start the noisy serenade which was sometimes called a "charivari" or "banding".

Some farmers brought their large circular wood cutting saw blades and wooden hammers to beat out an ear-spitting noise. Johnny Yingling had his trumpet and Jim Bachman had a horse fiddle braced up against the side of the house and was about to turn the crank to make a most ungodly vibrating sound for anyone still inside the house. One neighbor brought his shotgun to shoot in the air.

(cont'd)

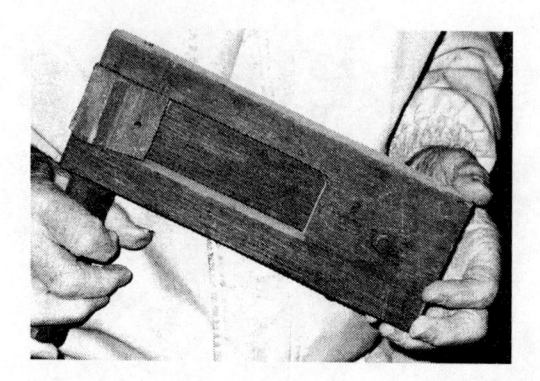

The wooden clapper which was swung around in the air was good for making lots of noise at a serenade.

Then most neighbors brought their largest buckets or old pans to beat with a stick as part of their contribution to the noisemaking.

Mr. Bitzel gave the sign to start the yard parade of noisemakers who would continuously walk around the house. It was very evident to Young George that Mary Bitzel and her new husband were still inside the Bitzel house. Once he believed he saw them peeking from around a curtain.

There was yelling, singing, and other taunts calling for the bride and groom to come out on the porch and take their medicine—that is, give a welcoming speech and invite everyone in to have cookies, cake and root beer. And so they did come out, after about six rounds of noisemaking. Mary, the new bride made a cute little welcoming speech. Sam was bashful and just raised his hand which meant "let's eat".

44

'Gees and Haws'

"There is a horse language—one that farm horses and mules understand. Four little words: gee, haw, whoa and giddy-up were taught to every colt broken to pull a wagon or plow. Horses and mules also understood the kind words their master spoke as they were being harnessed for the day's work."

Horses and mules cannot talk. But Young George wondered then why Papa and Grandpa were always talking to them in the stable when putting on their harness. They called it "horse language".

One day Young George asked Papa, "What does 'Gee' mean to old Bess?" Papa said, "Old Bess knows I want her to go to my right. If I say 'Haw', she knows to go left. 'Whoa' means I want her to stop, and 'Giddy-up' tells her to start moving." "But Grandpa showed me how to use the reins to guide Old Bess," Young George said. "You pull on the left rein to go left, and if you pull on the right rein, she will go right. He said you pull back on both lines for her to stop. Grandpa 'teached' me this one day when we were going to Bittinger's store."

Papa answered Young George, "If we talk to Old Bess, we don't have to pull on the reins. We can let them hang on the dashboard as we ride along in the buggy." Papa explained that while farm work horses and mules soon learn to obey these words it takes a lot of training for a new colt to understand what you want. He promised Young George he could help him train the next new colt they bought.

Grandpa always insisted that the lead horse in a team of two, three or four (even six sometimes) should be a good "Gee-Hawer". The lead horse was the left front horse in a team, and one who understood "Gee" and "Haw". All the horses knew "Whoa" and would stop on their own. When they heard "Giddy-up" they'd look at each other, nod and seem to step off together.

Papa told Young George more about horses. They knew their names. "If you use their name enough, they won't forget. That's why I call their names when I go in their stall and harness them up. When I say, 'Joe move over. Let's get your harness on,' Joe knows I'm beside him to throw on his harness. And he won't kick me or mash me up against the stall."

Grandpa always told Papa that yelling or beating a horse would ruin it. Papa was now teaching Young George these lessons. Some day he'd be old enough to drive a team hooked to a wagon by himself.

"GEE, PAPA! HAW, PAPA!"—Sometimes Papa or Mama would get hitched to a cultivator or plow to provide the "horse" power, and some laughs.

The Harness Shop

Among all the other skills a farmer had, he could also stitch and repair harness. Major repairs went to the harness maker.

"To get a horse ready to work, the farmer had to put a leather harness on the horse. Harness was fit for the maximum pulling power. But like anything else on the farm, harness wore out, broke and came apart. The harness maker, whether he be a farmer or craftsman skilled in making or repairing harness, was a necessary person for the farm."

Grandpa Shaffer spent a lot of winter hours repairing and oiling harness for the farm's six horses and mules while Young George looked over his shoulder. Actually, Grandpa was almost as skilled as any harness maker.

Usually in February each year, just before the "peeps" (baby chicks) came in the mail, Grandpa fired up the coal burning brooder stove in a room in one end of the chicken house to see if it was working and ready for the new chicks. It was warm in this little room, and on cold days in February he kept busy working on the harness. There was little else to do on the farm when it was bitter cold.

"Young George," Grandpa said, "How about you taking this harness oil as I bring the harness over from the barn and give it a good oiling. Then if there are any bad or worn parts, I'll cut out a piece from this new tanned leather from Sears Roebuck. And it'll look like new after I double sew it on the 'harness horse'."

(cont'd)

The old harness peg in the barn's horse stable was located so that the harness could be put on easily.

Young George soon asked his Grandpa, "You said you had to go to town to see Mr. Shunk about some harness." Grandpa said, "You're right, Young George. We'll go in soon to get two of our horse collars restuffed with straw. I don't do horse collars."

Fixing and oiling harness took almost a week of work in February each year. "You don't want any harness to break when you're busy hauling in the hay this summer," Grandpa said.

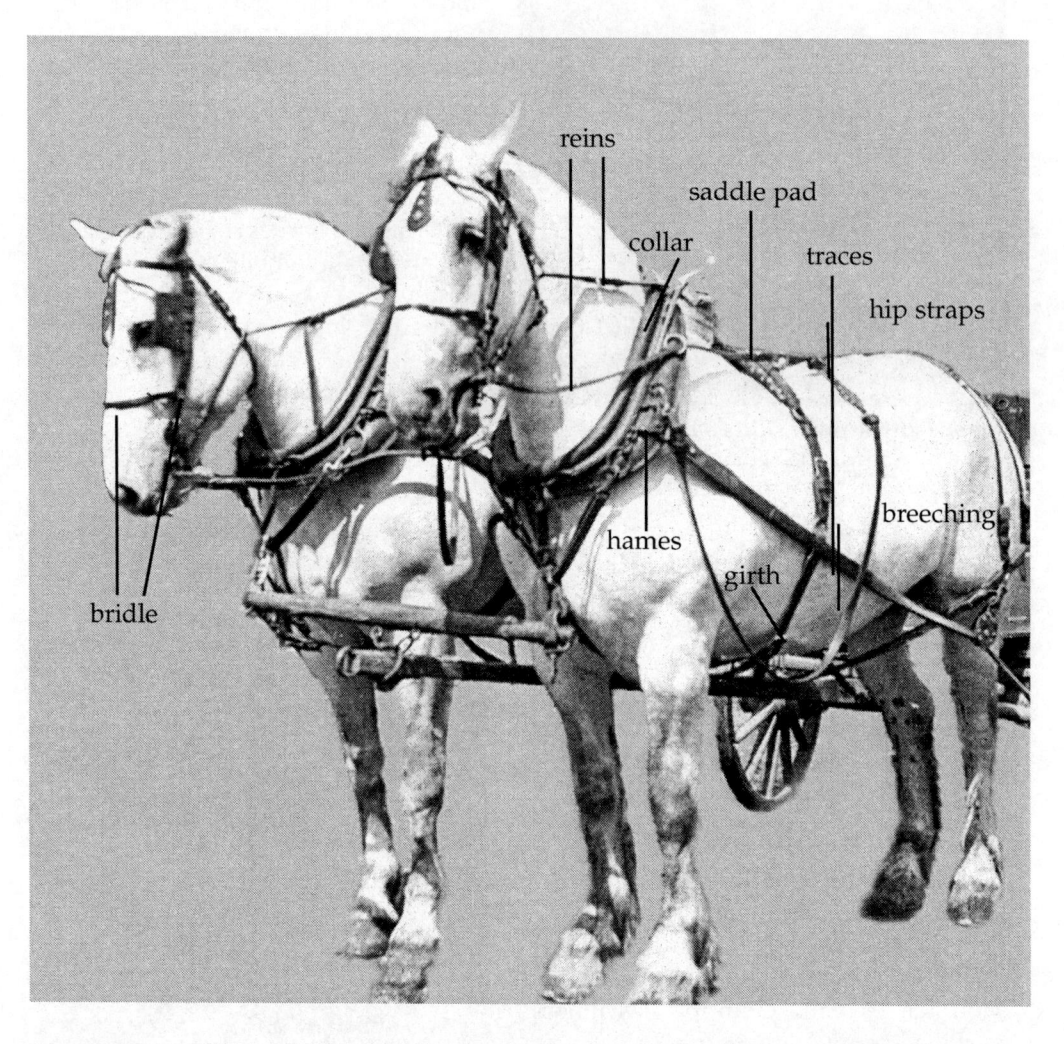

The parts of a harness all worked together in providing maximum pulling power from each horse and some comfort for the animals who would be required to work many hours in the fields. This two-horse rig is set up for a farm wagon. Similar harness was also used for a buggy.

48

Saturday Night Baths

"When Saturday nights came along on the farm, a must for farm kids was taking a warm water bath in the old wooden tub. The bath, with a bar of homemade lye soap, helped keep the kids clean for another week.

Immediately after supper on Saturday nights, Young George's Mama called for all the kettles and pots to be filled with water because Saturday night was the night the whole Shaffer family was scheduled for their weekly baths.

Young George's two sisters had gotten the kettles from the cellar. Young George and his Papa fetched the cold water from the spring and carried it to the kitchen in small buckets. Papa poured the water in the kettles and large pots on the old kitchen cook stove. Mama had made sure the stove was filled with good dry wood to heat the water in time for all the baths before their 8 o'clock bedtime.

Young George hated to take baths. The old wooden tub was hardly big enough for him to sit in. After all, he was almost four years old. Like most small boys on the farm, he couldn't see the same dirt his Mama said "was easy to see".

He usually said, "Mama, do I really have to take a bath tonight? Can I wait 'til tomorrow?" And she would say, "Get right in that tub, Young George. The warm water is in the tub, and here is a cloth to wash with. Look, don't splash the water out of the tub because your sister has to take a bath in your tub of water. Your towel is hanging on the back of the chair." If Young George had his way, he would wait until warm weather to take his bath.

The family left Young George in the kitchen, and he took off his pants, underpants, shoes and socks and climbed in the wooden wash tub of warm water his Mama had dipped from one of the kettles.

He took some of his Mama's homemade soap, smeared it on the cloth and started rubbing—feet first then up his legs, his bottom, his tummy, up to his neck and finally his face. Young George soon found the water getting cold, but the heat from the wood stove helped keep his backside warm.

(cont'd)

He finished his back, scrubbed his ears, then dipped his head in the tub of water to wash the hay seed out of his hair. He stepped out on the cold kitchen floor, grabbed the towel and started rubbing. And he was careful not to touch the hot stove.

After he was dry and had put on his warm clean clothes his mother laid out on a chair for him, Young George felt so good. He then called for his older sister, Helen, to take her bath then empty the tub of water out the kitchen door. When she had finished her bath it was time for the rest of the Shaffers to fill the tub and take theirs.

The kitchen cookstove is heating the kettles and pans of water while the wooden wash tub is waiting to do its weekly job of the Saturday night bath.

Young George climbed the crooked and creaking stairs and jumped into the deep, cold feather bed with a warm brick from the stove. He was asleep before he could get on his knees for his prayers.

In the summertime, there were times when Mama excused her requirement for the weekly bath if Young George and his sisters had been down to the creek for a swim. Maybe they had to wash their feet before they got into bed. To Young George that was better than taking a bath in that old wooden wash tub Mama used every Monday to wash clothes.

The John D. Roop family gathers for a family portrait, including their prized horses and mules, in the late 1800s on the Maryland farm now owned by the author and his wife. The wagon jack (below) was used to raise a wagon to remove a wheel.

There was always a "molasses barrel" in the country store along with a pot belly stove, coal oil barrel and "penny candy case".

51

The threshermen (left) pitch the sheaves of wheat into the threshing machine which separates the wheat seed from the straw. An orchardman (below) of the early 1900s sprays his fruit trees as a precaution against disease. A team of mules (bottom, right) pulls a drag across a plowed field to break up the clods of dirt. Corn was also run through this corn sheller (bottom, left) to provide chicken feed.

A Trip to the Mill

Barrels of flour are loaded on a wagon bound for market at the old brick grist mill at Union Mills, Maryland, built in the late 1700s.

"Most every farm boy at some time in his early life was able to talk his way into a wagon ride with his papa or grandpa to the local grist mill. His greatest treat was to see the miller lift the sluice gate and watch the water rush from the head race onto the large water wheel which turned from weight of the water. There were creaking noises as the machinery inside the mill turned to grind the corn or wheat."

Grandpa waited for a good summer day to take his grandson, Young George, down to the mill at Union Mills to get his corn ground for cattle, horse and hog feed. It was Young George's first trip to the mill. You would have thought it was his first trip to town he was so excited. Grandpa had used other mills in the area, but he wanted his grandson to see the large water wheel.

(cont'd)

They used the large wagon pulled by two of the old mules, Sam and Joe, who worked together as a team both in the field and on the road. Grandpa told Roger he wanted to take enough corn for a month's supply of chop for the cows, pigs and horses even though the cows were on pasture. He figured the cows would give more milk and the horses were facing some hard work.

It took 30 minutes for Sam and Joe to get that wagon down to the mill. The dirt roads were in good shape, and only one steep hill slowed them down. Grandpa had to stand on the wagon's "Lazy boy" wooden brake to keep the wagon loaded with corn from running over his mules.

They passed only two smaller wagons on the trip down, and, of course, Grandpa had to chat with each of the farmers. He would say, "How's yer corn crop gonna be this year?" To which there was the usual answer, "Don't know yet, but them ears seem to be filling out fair to midlin, what with a little rain."

Grandpa pulled up in front of the old mill and hooked a rope lowered down from the top of the mill. Each bag of corn was then lifted up to the second floor and was dumped into a hopper. The corn kernels were ground between the two buhrstones. One stone turned and one stayed still. Grandpa told Young George that there are two sets of these stones. One was for grinding wheat for flour—the other for corn meal.

(cont'd)

A millwright "sharpens" the buhrstone to allow for better milling of the corn or wheat. Another, opposing wheel sits on top of the buhr to create the grinding action on the flat surface of the stone. The ground corn meal or wheat flour drifts along the channels in the stone the millwright is cutting, and the centrifugal force moves the meal or flour to the outer edge of the stone where gravity carries it off through a series of wooden chutes to the awaiting barrels or cloth sacks.

The old mill was now over 100 years old. It was dusty, and Young George could hardly hear Grandpa shouting to the miller about what he needed.

"Can we go out to see that big water wheel, Grandpa?" They then walked across a little bridge over the head race that carried part of the water from Pipe Creek to the mill. Grandpa explained that the miller raises the sluice gate and lets water flow from the head race onto the big water wheel. The weight of the water makes the wheel turn. "That's what turns the machinery in the mill to grind the corn, wheat and buckwheat. The miller seems to be grinding for a lot of farmers today," Grandpa said.

Young George learned that his Mama's flour was made from wheat ground at the mill. Grandpa told him that one bushel of wheat makes 40 pound of flour. "Corn is also ground into corn meal that your Mama makes your corn cakes with for breakfast."

While at Union Mills, Grandpa and Young George visited the blacksmith nearby, then walked over to the tannery where cow hides were being cleaned and oak-tanned to be made into leather for shoes, harnesses and other leather goods.

(cont'd)

Wooden gears turn the mill machinery, including the buhrstone to grind the grain.

The sluice gate above this "overshot" wheel is partially lifted to allow water to surge into the buckets of the wheel which turns causing the gears inside the mill to also turn. This forces the buhrstones to turn against each other to grind the meal or flour.

Wagons are loaded with grain as farmers line up at the mill to have their sacks of grain unloaded by a pulley and hauled inside the old mill for grinding.

Young George found out they were not taking home as many bags as they brought. Grandpa quickly explained as they were loading up that the mill man did not take money from the farmers, but kept part of the corn (one-ninth of the total weight) as payment for the grinding work. This was the miller's "toll".

It was now up to these two mules to pull the big farm wagon back up the road toward the farm. Along the way, at the bottom of each hill, Grandpa would stop the wagon and let his mules rest before starting up another hill.

When Grandpa pulled the wagon into the barn, Papa was ready to unload the bags and carry them into the granary room where they could easily pour some of the grain through a hole in the barn floor at feeding time. Young George was busy telling Papa all about the mill and how the big water wheel turned the machinery inside the mill. He told the same stories to his mama and sisters at the supper table.

Chestnuts & Chinquapins

"When chestnut trees and chinquapin bushes grew, they provided farm families with a Sunday afternoon of nut gathering and fun in the fall—something no longer known.

The Shaffer's mighty chestnut trees were 80 feet tall. The chestnut tree had been the mainstay of farmers for several hundred years for timber to build their houses and barns. Its wood was rot-resistant and able to withstand the rains and snows for years. Some of the neighbor's barns had been built of chestnut boards and beams 100 years before. There was something else special about a chestnut tree.

Young George was just five years old and immediately understood what his Papa meant when he said, "Let's go hunt for chestnuts!" He barely remembered the last excursions out into the wooded grove at the far end of the farm on a previous chilly October morning looking for those sticky brown and green chestnut burrs. Young George also remembered cutting open the brown nut inside those burrs and liking their sweet taste.

What made it even more exciting was that the whole family walked down through the meadow, Mama, Papa, Mildred, Helen, and his young brother, Ralph.

Young George ran ahead as they aproached the woods and screamed, "The chestnuts down." That was his way of saying those sticky burrs had begun to fall and some were even opening up on the ground, and the large brown chestnuts were spilling out of the burrs.

Papa yelled, "While you're picking up the chestnuts in our tin buckets, I'll get a club and throw it up at some of the burrs still hanging on the trees, and knock a few more off. Mildred hollered, "Goody. I'll pick them up and stomp on them to get the burrs to open up, and I'll get baby Ralph to help me pick the chestnuts up and put them in our bucket."

Twenty years before, Grandpa Shaffer had cut one of his mighty chestnut trees for sawing boards to patch his barn and build a new chickenhouse. Grandpa said one of his trees would fill several railroad cars.

It didn't take long for the Shaffer family to fill their buckets with those sweet chestnuts.

(cont'd)

57

Papa showed Young George how to crack open the chestnut with a rock and then peel off the shell to eat the tasty chestnut meat. He said, "Young George. Your Mama will roast the chestnuts in the oven of the cook stove when we get back. Man, they sure will be good!"

Before they left the chestnut tree grove, Papa said to Mama, "Look at that one chestnut tree. It looks like it's dying at the top. The leaves are gone, and the bark is peeling off the top limbs. I"ve read that chestnut trees may have a blight and are dying. I hope the trees in our woods are not. I"ve got to bring Grandpa down to look."

Papa promised the girls he would take the family on a chinquapin hunt over at the Yingling farm the very next Sunday afternoon . The girls had gone over with some neighbors two years before, and this news brought squeals of delight from Mildred.

It didn't take long for the week to roll by, and Young George told his Papa he would help hook Old Bess to the milk wagon and put some straw in the back for the kids to sit on.

When the Shaffer family rounded the hill near the Yingling farm, they could see what seemed like a hundred people in the large Chinquapin grove filling their gallon lard buckets with those "small-like chestnuts" that were growing on bushes five to ten feet tall. Young George found immediately he could crack the small blackish-brown nuts with his teeth, and his mama warned, "Be sure to spit out the shell."

There were some 50 or more neighbors and even a number of persons from their church also enjoying the bright October afternoon sun. They all seemed to have buckets filled full of chinquapins. On the way home, Young George said, "Papa, I had fun today and also last week when we hunted for chestnuts. Let's do it again next year.

"It didn't take long for the Shaffer family to fill their buckets with those sweet chestnuts."

A Milk Cow's Dream

"Seven days a week, twice a day—there was a ritual known to all farm families who had dairy cows to be milked. No matter what the occasion—a farmers picnic or a Christmas dinner—the cows were expected to be milked before the evening sunset."

The Shaffers had an average of ten milk cows—mostly black and white Holsteins and always two or three reddish-brown Jersey cows. Papa liked the Holsteins because they gave more milk. Grandpa liked the Jerseys because the milk fat was greater and made more butter for Grandma and Mama to sell to Huckster Sam.

Because Grandpa and Papa treated their cows as if they were family, the Shaffers were considered to have one of the best herds in the valley. "Contented cows always give more milk," Grandpa said.

From the time he was one year old, Young George knew how to go "moo, moo." When Susie, the Jersey, was hooked in her stanchion she always raised her head for him to touch her slimy nose. After eating her evening "corn chop", she took her long pink tongue and tried to lick off the corn particles stuck to her nose and the side of her mouth.

As Young George grew he began to remember the names of each of the Shaffer cows as they walked through the stable door to be locked into their own self-chosen wooden stanchion to be fed and milked.

He would walk down the middle entry way between the horses and cows and call each cow by name. "Hi, Susie. Hi, Matilda, Lady, Lucy, May, Missy, Dolly, Lulu, Sally and Becky." If one of the cows got in the wrong place, he would scold her. And the next time, she would usually move to the right stanchion. Papa would then hook the stanchion shut to keep her in the right place as they milked.

Grandpa and Papa did most of the evening milking. Sometimes Mama would take Grandpa's place if he was not feeling well. After all, Mama had grown up on a farm too, and had been milking cows since she was a school girl. She had already seen to it that Young

(cont'd)

Sometimes cows were milked in the pasture to speed up the milking chore. Daughters were often recruited to do the milking.

George's sisters, Mildred and Helen, knew all there was about milking a cow. What if Papa got sick?

Young George had just finished throwing down the loose hay from the upper barn through the hole in the barn floor into the entryway below. His Papa called, Young George, get over here on the old wooden milk stool next to Lucy, and I'll teach you to milk." Lucy was one of the quietest cows and never kicked over a milk bucket while being milked. Some of the younger cows may have, if Young George sat down under their udders and in front of their back legs. Once before, Grandpa had let Young George squeeze one of Lucy's teats to show him where milk came from. He was only two years then, but now that he was almost four, Papa was getting him ready to help with the milking.

Old Lucy was calm and Young George had petted her on the head many times before, but now he was almost underneath her. And now the large tin bucket was between his small legs, and he sat on a milking stool that was barely one foot high. He was almost scared! Papa said, "You know how to milk using one hand—try it with two. First you squeeze with your right hand and then with your left. You have to milk and count—one and then two, one and then two. When you run out of milk in one teat, you go to the back teats and start all over again. Soon you'll have a bucket full of milk."

Young George told Papa, "Boy this makes your arms tired,"as he squirmed on his low milking stool. His bucket was almost half full of warm white milk, but he was only half finished with Lucy.

Tabby, the grey Maltese cat, came around next to Young George while he was taking his milking lesson.

(cont'd)

Tabby always got her warm milk at the barn. Young George would sit and wait for Papa to squeeze and point the stream of milk at her mouth instead of the bucket. There was a contented "Meow" of thanks from Tabby as she later finished her bowl of warm milk in the entryway away from the cows' hooves.

In the wintertime, it was usually dark when Young George and his Papa came from the barn. They used a lighted lantern hanging from a wire above the cows so they could see to finish milking and complete their feeding chores.

Once Papa filled a bucket with milk, he would pour and strain it into a five-gallon milk can which Mama had washed and carried to the barn. He then carried the full milk can to the spring house on a small, two-wheel cart and lifted it into the cool water. In the hot summer, Mama and the girls had to stir the milk at night. The next day, Papa and Grandpa would load the milk cans on the spring wagon and head down to the community milk stand. It was then taken to the railroad station to be shipped to the creamery in Baltimore. Mama made sure that enough milk was saved for cooking, the kids to drink and enough cream to make butter. In good weather the cows were driven out of the barnyard to the pasture. In the wintertime, they were kept in the warm barn or in the barnyard where they could munch on some fodder from the shocks hauled in from the cornfield.

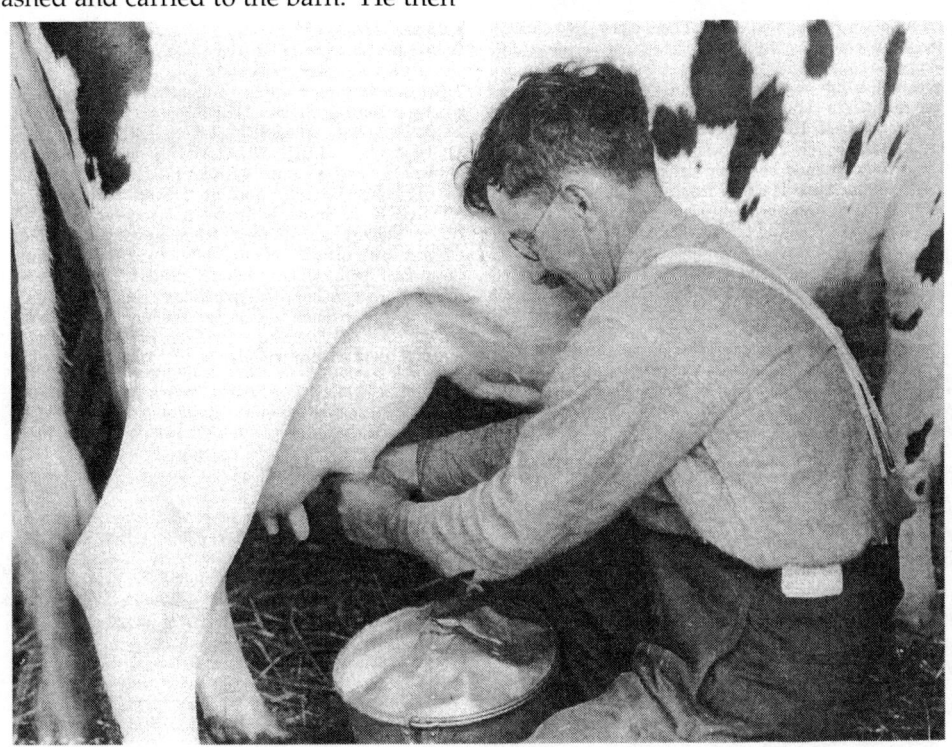

Milking was done by hand on the old farm—twice a day, seven days a week.

The Cold Room

The cold room was either a cave in the ground or a small building with thick stone walls. It was used to protect fruit and vegetables from freezing. This cold room was reportedly used during the Civil War.

"To a farmer, a cold room was a hole in the side of a hill that was covered with dirt or wooden planks. Sometimes it was a small building. Cold rooms could take the place of a cellar if the farmhouse didn't have one or if the cellar was too small for protecting all the fruit and vegetables from the winter freeze.

Grandma Shaffer knew their small farmhouse cellar was not large enough for all the vegetables and fruit she would want to keep over winter. So Grandpa built a cold room into the side of a dirt bank when the ice house was built. The cold room had heavy timbers on top, covered with three feet of earth and was eight feet long and six feet wide.

This hole in the ground was a favorite place for Young George to hide in the summertime when the cold room was empty and he was playing "hide and go seek". He called it the "cave". It had a door on the front that he could close. The cave also had a dirt floor with walls, and Papa could stand up inside.

Come October, it was time for Young George to help fill the cave with baskets of apples to be used during the winter months. In one corner they put their potatoes. He brought in carrots, beets and parsnips from the garden and covered them with sand. There were so many he may have some left for the horses and mules to eat.

Mama brought in her extra jars of canned goods that would not fit on the shelves in her cellar. She always said that apples kept in the cave tasted better and were crisper.

When colder weather came in November, Papa said, "Young George let's cover the cave with some fodder to make sure things won't freeze down under. We might even put six inches of loose straw over everything inside.

Cold Backs in the Winter

The old woodpile was kept close to the house, and the chopping block usually had a pile of split wood for the kids to carry into the kitchen woodbox.

Farm folk learned that the winter cold called for lots of dry wood to keep the fires burning hot all day. Even so, backing up to a red hot stove only warmed one side of you while the other stayed cold.

Winter wood was usually cut from the Shaffer's woods almost a year ahead. It needed to dry out and season in time for their stoves to keep the family warm as the snows began to blow.

The two Shaffer families kept the kitchen wood stoves burning almost year round for cooking their three meals a day. This meant the kitchen was too hot in the summer months even with the doors open but scarcely enough to warm the big kitchen room during the cold winter days.

Papa and Grandpa shared their wood from the large stack of logs cut and dragged in from the woods throughout the year. They also shared the job of cutting these logs into 18 inch stove lengths when they could spare a few hours from other farm work. They used a two-man cross-cut saw, and if they worked alone, a one-man saw.

(cont'd)

The next job at the woodshed was to split the logs in pieces for the kitchen woodstove and larger "chunks" to fit the big door in the living room stove.

Young George soon reached the age when his Papa let him try his hand at using an axe with a large hammer and wedge to split wood. He then piled it in a nice stack in the woodshed. Papa showed Young George how to be careful not to take any chances with a sharp axe and how to protect himself from flying wood or loose wedges.

Wood that's been cut in the woods is ready to be cut and split into stove length pieces.

When it came to carrying wood from the woodshed, Young George usually pleaded, "Mama, get Mildred and Helen to help bring the wood into the house." About half the time, Mama would say, "Young George. I have these girls cleaning the house and making beds. You'll have to finish that job yourself today."

Most of the Shaffer's firewood was oak and hickory which made the hottest fires and didn't burn too fast. Occasionally they would cut a dead chestnut tree. It split more easily into thin strips that could be used to start their morning fires with a douse of coal oil or newspaper. Papa would not let the kids do the fire starting for he was afraid they would use too much coal oil and start a chimney or house fire.

The girls and Young George usually did their studying around the kitchen table under the dimly-lit coal oil lamp. The kitchen was already warm because the stove had been burning all day.

In the room the Shaffer family called their living room, Papa would light the fire before supper time, and it was usually warm enough for the entire family to pull up a chair around the old chunk stove after they had eaten. Here he read passages from the Bible before they started their school lessons in the kitchen.

Young George usually sat on the floor next to the living room stove before bedtime to warm his back. If that side of the stove started to get red hot, Mama Mary would yell, "Young George. You're going to catch your shirt on fire. Move!"

On top of either the kitchen or living room stoves there were always some bricks or pieces of soapstone warming to be wrapped in cloth and taken up to bed as a footwarmer in an ice cold bedroom and bed.

A Fence or Two

"Fences were about the only way farmers kept their horses and cattle home on the farm or their neighbor's cattle from coming in and ruining a corn crop. Fences of all types were created by farmers to accomplish these purposes."

Young George was watching Grandpa and Papa cut down some of their chestnut trees one cold winter day. Remembering the fall days when they gathered chestnuts, he asked Grandpa why he was cutting down his chestnut trees.

Grandpa took Young George over to one of the logs, sat down, and said, "Young George, how are we going to keep our cows in our pasture field if we don't build a new fence? This chestnut log we are sitting on will make twelve rails when we split it the right way, and this chestnut wood will last for years. It's the best fence we can put up."

"When you study about Abraham Lincoln, one of our presidents, you will find out he was a good rail splitter when he was growing up on a farm."

Farmers around were aware of a new "barbed" wire fence that an Illinois farmer named Joe Glidden had designed in 1874. True, it was now being offered in some of the local hardware stores, but as long as the chestnut tree was around, most would stick with the old "Worm-split rail" fence. It was easy to erect and always a good winter time job. Sometimes, a farmer would put the rails between posts (a post and rail fence) which some considered more effective against heavier cattle and horses. Grandpa, during their next break in the sawing and splitting job, gave Young

(cont'd)

65

George a little more fence information. "You know at the far end of our back field which is "boney" with rocks—over the years we've built a stone wall from rock we gathered from our fields and the woods we cleared to make more farmland. A lot of farmers have stone fences like that. At least they will never rot."

Papa chipped in on the conversation and reminded Grandpa that Sam Baumgardner had used stumps left over from clearing his wooded area and dragged them out along his field to make a "stump fence". Stumps with their roots stacked side by side made a good fence that cows or horses could not get through.

Most farmers who had a chestnut grove, cut and sold their rails to other farmers for fencing. Grandpa told Young George that soon there would be the need to cut chestnut trees to make poles to put new telephone lines along roads leading to farms. That may be a little while, but the telephone is coming. I believe we can get more money from our chestnut trees for poles rather than selling as chestnut rails.

There is no doubt the wire fence with its "sticky" barbs will be the thing of the future for farms like ours. You would then have to cut and dig holes for the locust posts. We might try it some day."

The stone fence (above) was popular where a farmer had excess stones in his fields to pick up. The stump fence (below) came about during the clearing of land where stumps were pulled together to make a fence. Rail fences (left) of all types were popular, though the post and rail probably was the most reliable.

The Country Blacksmith

"The blacksmith was a necessity in farm life—much like a farmer's horse or cow. It was the shoes for a horse or a steel rim for a wagon wheel that he made. By the end of any day, a "Smithy" may have shoed 18 horses."

In the corner of the farm shed, Grandpa had an old forge and an anvil along with a variety of tongs and chisels. He was capable of fixing many things that a blacksmith could such as repairing a broken hinge, or welding a piece of metal for holding the corner of a wagonbed together. But there were many jobs that a blacksmith did which Grandpa wouldn't touch like shoeing a horse, making a chain or repairing a rim on one of his wagon wheels. These were jobs for old Mac in his blacksmith shop near town.

Grandpa had long taught Roger to keep his eye on his horses' hooves to see if there were any loose or lost horse shoes, or whether they were wearing too much thus preventing them from getting a good grip in the mud if they were pulling a heavy load.

On a cold March day, Grandpa asked Roger to take old Bess and Maude down to old Mac for a "shoeing job". And that was the same day three or four other farmers decided to do the same thing. There were six horses ahead of him. That meant at least a couple of hours to trim and nail on new shoes before the blacksmith could get to Bess and Maude. Roger decided to wait and entered into "crop talk" with the farmers standing around the old shop.

When it was Roger's time to bring in Old Bess he stood and watched Mac pry off the iron shoes and get out his nippers and knives and start trimming the edges of old Bess's brittle hooves. Mac said, "Roger, you've been usin' old Bess a good bit, ain't you?" Roger said, "She's my choice driving horse

(cont'd)

A good blacksmith could shoe nearly 20 horses each day. Horseshoes had to be heated, fitted and nailed on the horse's hooves after they were trimmed.

Inside a typical blacksmith shop at the turn of the 1900s, the "smithy" works at his anvil—the most used of his equipment. The shop is filled literally ceiling to floor with horseshoes waiting to be sized and fitted along with hundreds of tongs, each used for a specific job.

As Old Mac worked he asked, "Roger, did you ever hear of a blacksmith named John Deere? He made a steel plow by taking an old saw blade and using it to mold a new plow design with the right curve, a sharp point and leading edge. That single-bottom walking plow with its polished surface cut through the toughest grass. It's still used by hundreds of you farmers."

Roger watched Old Mac pull on the bellows handle to pump more air into the forge for a hotter fire to get the last horseshoe red hot for bending on the anvil to fit Maude's left hind hoof. When he was satisfied with the shape and fit he plunged the shoe in the water tub to cool. Then he nailed it on.

Roger asked, "How come you can get under a horse, hold its hoof in your leather apron on your lap and not get kicked?" Old Mac said, "Those horses that do kick, know I gotta a sling over there that will pick them up off the floor while I work and that they can't kick a lick when they're up there in that sling. It probably does take a kick or two before I know which horses to start off in the sling."

While shoeing took most of Old Mac's time, he kept busy heating, tightening and fitting rims on wagon and buggy wheels. The mud and rough roads loosened not only the spokes, hubs and rims, but it often broke a metal rim or the wheel itself. But the blacksmith was the one who could get a wagon back on the road again.

A Visit From Huckster Sam

"The huckster was a necessary part of farm life. It was he who bought the farmers' butter and eggs and brought with him the news of the community."

In the last years of the 1890s and the first part of the 1900s, the Shaffer family waited for the weekly visit from Sam—a well known huckster. He could almost be counted upon to be at the farm at 11 o'clock each Wednesday.

Sam drove his covered wagon (or covered sled during the winter snows) over the mud and dirt roads to buy eggs and butter from farmers to deliver to his Baltimore customers. He would say to Grandma Martha, "I bet you have an extra dozen chickens you'll sell me. Good price—thirty five cents today."

Sometimes Papa and Grandpa would sell a calf for ten dollars or a goat for four dollars. If there was an extra bushel of green beans in the summer,

(cont'd)

A huckster pays the farmer's wife for the butter and eggs he's just bought from her.

after he reached Baltimore. If he did not finish his city huckster route, he spent the night in a hotel, Huckster Sam always loaded up his wagon for the trip back, mostly with supplies ordered by country storekeepers. These items would include barrels of molasses, sugar, and other staples. On his trip back from the city, Huckster Sam would stop on the way and sell other items he had purchased.

Sam would buy them. Any chickens that Grandma sold were ones that weren't laying well. While in the area, Huckster Sam visited the Snyder, Bixler and Orndorff farms before he reached the Shaffer farm. By the end of the day he probably had gotten around to the Everhart, Stonesifer, Bachman and Warehime farms. He tried to visit farms within six or seven miles from his home north of town.

When Young George reached the age of five he could climb around the rafters of the barn and catch some pigeon squabs, and get 25 cents each from Huckster Sam. In the winter months he would have an occasional muskrat or rabbit which he had caught and earned another 25 cents each.

Most hucksters upon arriving back at their homes, cleaned and crated the eggs, cut the rolls of butter gotten from the farmers into one pound pieces and wrapped them in paper. He killed, cleaned and dressed his chickens before starting for his trip to Baltimore. Huckster Sam drove his wagon to the city in good weather, but in the winter months often put his load on the train at 6 a.m. He rented a horse and wagon

Huckstering was a necessary business for the farm wife and her family. It was the huckster who helped her pay the farm mortgage.

The huckster's sled was used when the snows were too deep for the wagon to reach the farmers.

70

The New Penknife

It was a young farm boy's dream to carry his first penknife in his pocket. He could then whittle or make a bow and arrow and be a "somebody" in school just like most farm boys who cut their initials in the top of their wooden school desks."

Young George was approaching his fifth birthday when Grandpa Shaffer called to him as he was going into the barn. "Oh, Young George, Grandpa wants to talk with ye. Come on over to our house."

(cont'd)

Young boys, and old ones too, carried a penknife, for just whittlin' or making a new whistle.

Usually when Grandpa called, Young George had a pretty good idea it was important. So he did not waste any time getting across to Grandpa's house.

"You know, Young George. I think your birthday is Friday. Five years old ye be. I have a present I bought down at the new hardware store in town. Open it up. Let's see what 'tis." Young George tore open the little black box and his eyes widened as he saw a real penknife—almost like his Papa's. "Boy, Grandpa, thanks. I need a penknife here on the farm. Now I can cut twine just like you and Papa."

"Now look here, Young George. We're going to have a lesson or two so you won't cut off one of your fingers. Go show your Mama and Papa your knife, and tomorrow you come over, and we'll go down to the woods and cut a chestnut sucker, and I'll show you how to make a real wooden whistle." Young George was bubbling over when he showed his new present from Grandpa. His Mama frowned at his having such a large, sharp knife. "Roger, you have to show Young George how to use that knife. I don't want any bloody fingers around here. Roger said, "Between Grandpa and myself, we'll take care of the lessons. Young George is going with Grandpa to make his first whistle."

The next morning Young George was over at Grandpa's bright and early. Almost too early, for Grandpa had not finished up the stack of corn cakes Grandma had brought over from the old cook stove.

The two wandered down through the meadow—a sixty two-year-old and the other five years of age—in search of a sucker limb from a chestnut stump. Grandpa said it had to be about two inches thick and long enough to make a dozen wooden whistles, six to eight inches long.

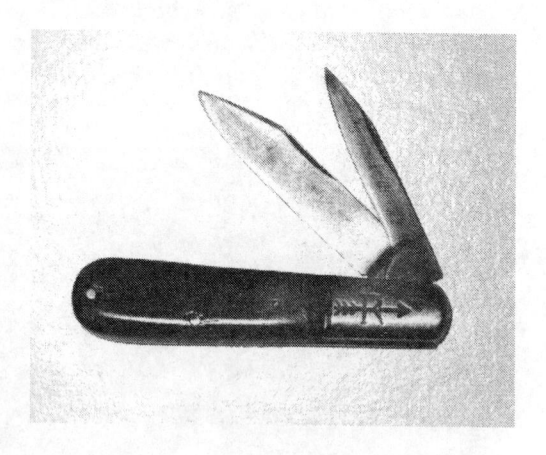

Grandpa showed Young George how to hold the knife and cut off the small limb—always cutting away from his body with that sharp, new penknife. Grandpa had made whistles a lot of times when his own kids were growing up. He helped Young George cut off a half dozen pieces from the limb. "Now comes the trick, young fella. We have to rub the bark hard and cut it so that half of the bark slides off the stick. Then we cut a sliver of wood from where the bark was, and a notch in the middle before we slide the bark back on. It's ready now to blow through, and the notch makes it whistle. The smaller the notch, the higher the whistle sound."

"I think I can now make one all by myself," Young George said. That night at the supper table he blew his new whistle, and told his sisters he'd be making them one too.

Feeding Time at the Barn

Chopped corn fodder was sometimes fed to the herd when pasture grasses were short.

"Cows took up most of the space in the lower part of the farmer's barn—cows, calves and heifers. For the most part, their milk paid the farmer's bills and his farm mortgage. It was important that they be fed. But that didn't mean the farm work horses, mules and pigs could be forgotten. They, too, ate a lot—two times a day, seven days a week."

Young George was glad his Papa needed him at the barn. Soon he would be one of the right-hand men in the morning and evening feeding chores. After all, Grandpa was getting older and would soon be giving up some of the work.

Two years earlier, when Young George was three, he was large enough to go into the calf pen with Papa to help teach a new calf to drink warm new milk from a bucket. Papa taught him to let the small calf suck on his forefingers, and at the same time lower his fingers down into the milk. It wasn't long before he had that calf drinking from the bucket without his help. This was a job he would be teaching his young brother, Ralph. Sisters Mildred and Helen already knew that part of calf feeding chores.

Let's see. There were six horses, two mules, 12 cows and a dozen heifers in the barnyard, plus five or six young calves in the calf pen to feed. Papa usually fed the heifers which ran loose out in the barnyard. He was afraid Young George would get run over as they rushed to get their hay which he spread around in the yard.

Calf feeding was just a small part of the evening and morning work at the barn. Each night it was necessary to go up in the hay loft and throw down loose hay onto the upper barn floor. It was then pitched through a chute to the entryway between horses and cattle.

(cont'd)

From the corn crib, the men usually carried over to the barn a few bushel baskets of the yellow ear corn. Young George's job was to see that each of the horses and mules got about three ears in their feed box where he watched as those big white teeth shelled the corn off the cob. He noticed old Bess's teeth were getting short, and she was having a hard time shelling hers. He would take an ear and shell it for her. He was sure her short neighing sound was to "thank" him

As the cows were about to be milked by Papa and Grandpa, Young George gave each cow a scoopful of corn chop that had been ground at the mill and mixed with some bran. After they were milked, he gave each cow a small pitchfork of clover hay. The horses were now whinnying and prancing around in their stalls, and he put a forkful of timothy hay in their racks, being careful not to stick the fork in their faces.

During the warmer weather in the spring, summer and fall months, Papa turned the cows and horses out in the pasture for the night and during the day to munch on the green pasture grasses. It meant many times that Young George and the kids had to drive the cows up to the barn in time for the morning and evening milkings.

The pigs, which were in the small building with an open pig pen next to the barn, were the last to be fed. Much of their food came from the "slop bucket" which contained food scraps, potato peels, rotten apples and dish water. Papa usually carried the day's slop bucket as he went to the barn. Sometimes Mama had extra buttermilk that was not used, and this was added to the pigs' food as was the middlings or "shorts" brought from the mill.

Young George liked to sit on the fence while Papa was pouring the pigs' meal in their trough. He delighted in seeing the scrambling and pushing, and hearing the grunting and squealing pigs trying to beat each other slopping up their food. Once in awhile, there was a "runt" because he could not force his way to the food trough, and Young George saw to it that he got some food on the side.

In the early mornings, Young George would always say to Papa after the feeding and milking, "Boy, I'm ready for those hot cakes and sausage. We really worked hard this morning." It was the same conversation at night as he walked back from the barn to the house with Papa. "Papa, Mama's got a good meal waiting for us. Let's get in the house. I'm hungry."

Peddlers, Tramps and the Like

"Most farm lanes in the countryside were an open invitation for peddlers, tramps and gypsies to see if they could get a cup of coffee or sell something to the farmer's wife. They came by foot (in the case of the wandering tramp) or by horse and wagon loaded with wares the peddlers or gypsies had made."

A "tramp" has a bit of luck with a cup of coffee from a farm wife.

Young George was used to seeing Sam, the Huckster, come to the farm every Wednesday for butter, eggs, or an occasional chicken or calf. But if he saw a stranger coming down the lane, he would run to the house and holler, "Mama, there's a strange man coming in our lane. It could be the pottery peddler who came every year or so. Or it could be a tramp looking for a meal or a cup of coffee in exchange for some work.

Every spring Grandma and Mama would look for the pottery man who traveled in his loaded wagon pulled by two horses. It was his custom to spend two or three days away from his pottery kiln in Pennsylvania soliciting orders and cultivating goodwill with his farmer patrons.

The pottery man carried with him many items of stone, earthen and Rockingham ware. There would be milk pans, pitchers, chicken fountains, earthenware crocks, stove pipe guards, flower pots and spittoons. The average cost for these items ran from a few cents to $1.50 for a five-gallon jug.

Tramps roamed the roads and by-ways in good weather. Sometimes they moved on after a cup of coffee or maybe slept in the barn at night and were given a meal by Mama. Young George liked tramps because they usually had stories to tell, or they saved him from having to split stove wood.

But Young George had been warned to watch out for the gypsies. Bands of gypsy families traveled in their fancy wagons and sold articles they had made. Grandpa said he'd heard of gypsies who had stolen chickens, and friends of Young George said they would hide under their beds for fear of being stolen by gypsies.

| Dog | Keep Quiet | Very Good | Bad Dog |

"Tramps" made signs they would scratch on fences to warn future travelers.

Apples Grow On Trees

Farmers took their apples to the cider mill each fall, but the best apples were saved for apple butter.

"Nearly every farmer and his wife would plant a small, two or three-acre corner on their farm in fruit trees. This was their orchard, and it provided apples for their apple butter; filled their colorful fruit jars and sent their kids off to school with a big red apple in their lunch boxes, with an extra for the teacher."

In the fall of 1877 Grandpa was looking at a copy of "The Advocate" newspaper and saw an advertisement for a new nursery outside of town owned by a Mr. Stout. He had fruit trees for sale as well as grape vines, blackberries, raspberries, gooseberries, strawberries and currants.

Early the next spring, Grandpa took his spring wagon, his ten-year-old son Roger, and made the two-hour trip across country to Mr. Stout's nursery to buy some trees. Roger was on his first trip to a large town, and was equally excited about Mr. Stout digging up the small three-foot apple trees and putting them on Grandpa's wagon. Grandpa had strict orders from Grandma to get the kind of trees that made good apple butter. He chose some Yorks, Staymans, Smokehouse and a larger greenish-red apple called Summer Rambo. He also bought a cherry tree, peach tree and 100 strawberry plants. The trees cost $3.35 and the strawberry plants were a quarter.

Martha Shaffer wanted to know all about Roger's trip. After all, her boys never got off the farm except when they went to church or the little log school house on the Baumgardner farm.

Grandpa Shaffer had set aside a little hillside back of the barn for the orchard. It was well-drained, but too hilly to be running a plow over for any crops. He put a fence around it, and eventually used it to run his heifers and calves for pasture before the apples started to drop in late summer.

Grandpa and the boys planted the fruit trees on the hillside, and it was Roger's job to carry a bucket of water from the spring and put on each tree. Grandpa told him it would be his job to care for the trees as they grew. He would water them, put manure around them and trim the branches each year.

When Young George was born 16 years later and old enough to wander

(cont'd)

The cider always had to be tested, and there was never a shortage of testers to sip the sweet cider through a barley or wheat straw.

around and talk, his Papa told him about his trip some 20 years earlier with grandpa to buy the apple trees for the orchard. He told him how small they were when he helped plant them. The trees were now 30 feet tall and already several had to be cut down for firewood. Grandpa had told Roger it was his job to take care of the orchard, and now Roger was telling Young George it would be his job too some day, and maybe plant new trees as the old ones died.

In the fall, the entire family gathered in the orchard to pick up the apples that were falling. The unbruised ones were carried to the cellar until it was time to pare and cut them up for making apple butter. Already, Roger had taken a load of fallen apples down to Johnny Weller's cider mill to make cider. Young George fed some of the apples which were "knotty" and rotting to the hogs.

The kids, young and "old", always like to take barley straws and sip the sweet apple juice (cider) from the bung hole in the side of the big wooden barrel. A week or so later, as the cider "hardened", Grandpa got caught sipping it from the barrel. He always said, "You kids stay away from this barrel. It's getting hard, and your Mama is putting in 'mother' (bacterial cells from old vinegar) for making the cider turn to vinegar." From then on, Mama had charge of the cider barrel and would soon be drawing vinegar for her butchering and other farm cooking needs.

A team of four horses pulls a harrow to work up a cornfield prior to the fall wheat planting.

Horses Versus Mules

"Farmers have argued for centuries whether horses or mules made the best farm work teams. None won the argument because those who had horses swore by a horse's common sense while the owners of mules were just as sure their mules could outlast their neighbor's horse on a hot summer day."

Before he was two years old, Young George could tell Grandpa which was a horse and which was a mule. "Big ears on mule," he would tell Grandpa.

The mule being a cross between a female horse and a donkey (jack) looks like both parents—long ears, short mane and small feet from the jack. From the horse, the mule gains a well-shaped body and strong mind. The horse is a thing of beauty, whether a driving horse or draft horse with their large feet and thick bodies.

The Shaffers had two mules to go with their four work horses. The mules worked as well with the two horses in a four-horse team as they did behind a plow by themselves. Grandpa had always told Papa, "It's all in how young mules were broken to work farm equipment as to whether they were a cantankerous blankety blank animal or whether they were quiet and 'non-kickers' when you went into their stalls to put on their harness."

Most farmers found that a horse has all kinds of "horse sense". They might have one-track minds, yet the horse possesses a terrific memory and responds to firm, but consistent, treatment. He can easily be taught to do things when the farmer uses extreme patience and repetition. Papa Shaffer told Young George, "The carrot and not the whip brings good horse work habits."

(cont'd)

Three mules and one horse are pulling a manure spreader (above). The same team awaits the "get-up" order (below) before heading out to the field.

In a likeness to people, some horses are timid. Some are stand-offish, and some are very friendly and affectionate. They all respond well, however, to any rewards given them for excellent work. A good driving horse could pull a buggy eight to ten miles in one hour.

Papa Shaffer liked both the horse and the mule. He sometimes blessed his mules if they had a stubborn streak and didn't want to work after the dinner bell.

On the other hand, he liked a mule's smaller feet because they were sure-footed and didn't trample as much corn when he was pulling a cultivator. In the extreme hot weather he could also see his mules worked slower—drank less water than his horses, and ate less food.

Regardless, both animals are a farmer's best friend in front of a plow or wagon.

No doubt this team of three mules and one horse pulled their own weight with this hook-up.

One Potato, Two Potato

"Every farm had a potato patch—one which fed the farm family all through the year and, perhaps, brought in some spare cash if the crop was a good one."

Potatoes were a food staple that was found on the farm table at least two meals each day. A farmer's wife was adept to cooking potatoes in a variety of ways to insure that, along with meat and a couple vegetables, it kept her man and kids in shape for a hard day's work.

(cont'd)

Mama Shaffer was taught by Grandma to fry potatoes, boil potatoes, mash potatoes, as well as how to make potato soup, scalloped potatoes and potato salad. Then there were baked potatoes, stewed potatoes, potato cakes, potato pies and potato bread.

Papa had taken over Grandpa's job of planting and digging two potato crops each year. It was his decision as to the size of the patch for the early potatoes, and then in July he would decide whether he needed a larger patch for the late crop. The whole family was engaged in the planting and digging jobs. It usually took two days for Grandpa to cut the seed potatoes he had kept over the winter. He had an old box in the cellar where he sat and cut each potato into pieces so that there were at least two "eyes" in each portion of the seed potato. He usually ended up with about ten bushels for planting each crop.

Young George wondered why the "potato eyes" were so important and Grandpa said, "Each eye in the piece of potato becomes a potato plant, and when that plant grows, new little potatoes grow on its roots. When the potatoes get fairly large, you can see them pushing up the ground, and you know it's time to dig them up."

In March Papa usually tried to have the potato patch plowed, worked up and the old shovel plow dusted off ready to plow a 12-inch deep trench for each row across the patch. Young George, along with his sisters and Mama were pressed into service to drop Grandpa's "cut-up" potatoes in the trench about 10 to 12 inches apart. It was a back-breaking job, and Young George always told his Mama that his back hurt. She would tell him, "Wait 'til these potatoes grow, and we have to dig them and pick them up in the heat of July. Then your back will really hurt."

The early crop was what Papa called his "new potatoes" (early white potatoes). His late potato crop was planted in July, and he called those the "Dakota Reds". This year he planned on planting about half a acre of each kind. He figured this would be enough to feed the two families and have some potatoes to sell.

Digging the early white potatoes was usually done in mid July or after the vines had died. By then Young George noticed that the ground was "heaving up", and he knew it was time for Papa to get the shovel plow, and one of the old mules harnessed to pull the plow.

Despite the fact that most of the potatoes were pulled out on top of the ground with the shovel plow, he had to use the potato fork to find them all. Young George found out picking up potatoes was a "back-breaking" job for kids. They had to dump their buckets full of potatoes into bags and baskets before hauling them down to Grandpa's house where they put them in the empty potato bins in the cellar, or out in the cold room. The bins were built of rough lumber to keep the potatoes off the floor so they wouldn't rot.

The red potatoes that Grandpa cut up were planted in July and were usually ready to dig in September or early October. Papa covered Grandpa's seed potatoes using the shovel plow. He cultivated them during the summer to keep the weeds out. Young George soon found out that he had to pull a lot of large weeds that the cultivator missed.

Huckster Sam kept his eyes on both plantings of potatoes and was all smiles when he saw that the Shaffers were going to have a good potato crop. He knew also that Papa would probably sell him a few bushels each week for his customers.

1-Room School + 3R's

School is in session in a one-room school. Note the pot belly stove and double school seats.

"Readin', ritin' and 'rithmetic were basic to the one-room school as was the big black potbelly stove. Barefooted kids shooting marbles and no school buses were the sign of the times in 1900."

Young George Shaffer was six years old when he started attending the one-room school two miles down the road from the farm. The morning was crispy cool, and it was September 1900.

He had been excited all week about going to school with his sisters, Mildred and Helen, who had been attending the school for almost five years. He had gone with them to school once when he was four on visitor's day.

"I'll be ready to leave at seven o'clock tomorrow morning," he told Mama the night before. "I've got my new yellow pencil and tablet and my new round lunch pail. I'll wear my new blue pants you made for me. Will you have my lunch ready before I get back from the barn, Mama, jus' so we won't be late on the first day of school?"

On that fateful morning, Young George went to the barn with Papa and finished his chores of feeding the cows and horses earlier than usual and headed back to the house for breakfast.

(cont'd)

Mama had his sausage and corn cakes ready on the cook stove. He barely ate, and his sister Mildred teased him about being afraid to face Mrs. Brown, the teacher at Backwoods School.

"Let's go," Young George coaxed. "We'll be late and Mrs. Brown will be mad." And away the Shaffer kids went in their barefeet. It was down the long dusty lane and then two miles down the dirt road to school. Young George knew that he did not have to put on shoes until corn cutting time in October. .

It took about 40 minutes to make the walk. Three neighboring Wolfe kids joined in, and as they neared the schoolhouse the bell was ringing from the belfry on top of the school. Mildred said that was a five minute warning, and they all would be in time for the final bell.

Mrs. Brown welcomed the 32 new students and led them in saying the Lord's Prayer. Young George was excited and waved to his sisters sitting across the room in their double wide seats. He was in the first grade, and he counted seven other boys and girls in his class. Mrs. Brown had each of the first graders introduce themselves and gave each a new reader for them to take home and look at the first four pages. The reader was called "The Little Red Hen". It was recitation time, and Young George and the rest of the first graders were just to listen to the others.

His favorite was recited by an

The one-room school with vestibule and belfry was home to "readin', ritin' and 'rithmetic".

older boy: "*Shoe the colt, shoe the mare, let the little colt go bare.*" Then there was another short one he would remember: "*Lemon, lemon, lemon lime—lemon, lemon, be on time.*"

There was a large potbellied stove in the middle of the school room. A well-worn coal bucket sat beside the stove on the wooden floor. Young George kept turning around in his seat watching and listening to Mrs. Brown talking to the second grade about reviewing multiplication tables. He believed he would like to know what two and two was. He could do it by using his fingers but made up his mind he would remember it like those second graders did.

At 10:30 the teacher said everyone in the school would have to take "recess" which Young George found to be "playtime". He and the first graders watched the games the big kids were playing. One game called "Kaddy" looked strange to Young George. They would take a long stick and hit down on a small pointed piece of wood with numbers on the sides. It would fly up in the air and the side facing up with a number when it hit the ground was what counted. Then the next boy would take his turn. On the other side of the school girls were playing "dodgeball".

The bell rang and Mrs. Brown started down the other side of the room. It was Mildred's sixth grade, and Young George wanted to know how hard her lessons were going to be. There were only nine in her class.
The teacher was talking about President McKinley and about Teddy Roosevelt being the next president. He would ask Mildred more about that going home. Young George took his new shiny lunch pail off the shelf in the outdoor vestibule room and found his sister Helen who took him outside and over to sit on the roots of a large gum tree in the schoolyard. There they ate the sandwiches Mama had packed for them and finished with an apple from their farm.

The rest of the lunch hour had Young George watching the older boys throwing a rubber ball over the roof of the school and calling "Ante Over". If they caught it on the fly they rushed around the school and yelled, "Halt", and tried to hit the closest opponent with the soft rubber ball. If he was hit, he declared "out" and had to stop playing. If one side had no players left, the other team won.

There were only three or four six and seventh graders—all girls. Mildred told Young George the boys work on their family farms until the weather gets cold. She told him, "The boys come to school only in the winter, but in March or April when the plowing starts, they stop school again."

If it rained hard, Papa or Mama sometimes hooked Ole Bess to the buggy and took them to school. Young George noticed that two or three kids even rode a horse to school, and they would let it loose to find its way home by itself.

Butchering Days

"The farm family in 1900 probably depended more on butchering days for its food than was provided by any other activity. Each family raised five to ten hogs and a steer or two for butchering."

Butchering time brought the farm community together in the dead of winter in order to provide the meat supply for the entire year.

Young George was three when he first watched the Shaffer family butcher the hogs. At that age he was almost too small to be of much help, much less remember what was going on.

But in the next few years, long before butchering day, he would say, "Papa, can I help butcher hogs this time? I'm big now—six years old." Papa replied, "Young George. I'll let you help this winter, but only when I'm with you. The rest of the time you stand clear. It's dangerous work, and I don't want you to get hurt."

Around Thanksgiving Day the weather determined when farmers looked forward to getting their butchering out of the way. Some farmers butchered again in January. During the cold part of the winter season most farmers butchered a steer. Grandpa Shaffer had for a long time butchered five or six hogs that he raised. He wanted good hams and had fattened his hogs slowly. All the old plowshares, pieces of metal, and large stones from the pile kept from the previous years would be put on the fire built to get them red hot early on butchering day.

Also the day before butchering, the old tables used for cutting up the meat had to be cleaned. Knives had to be sharpened. And tripods, hooks and gambling sticks, all used to hang up the hog carcasses, needed to be readied for the next day. The large barrel used to scald the hogs was scoured and filled with water ready for the hot iron and stone to be thrown in the next morning. And of course, head butcher Henry Rupp and his helper, had been notified to be at the Shaffer farm the day after Thanksgiving.

This farmer has his work cut out for him with a large number of hogs ready for butchering.

Farmers often used a head butcher to help with the hard part of butchering and to insure that the right ingredients were added to the meats for the curing process. The fire was started at 2 a.m., and Young George helped Papa carry plow shares over to be put on the fire now burning briskly.

Henry Rupp and his helper went down to the pig pen next to the barn and soon had the first dead pig ready to slide into the barrel of scalding water. Henry used a corn cob to dip into the hot water and said to young George, "If I can hold the corn cob, the water is too cold, and I'll tell your papa to throw in another red hot plow share to make the water hotter. This will soften up the dead pig's hair when we slide him off these boards into the barrel. We can then bring him out and scrape his bristles off.

The gambling sticks were used to hang the hog up by its hind legs on those tripods in the wagon shed. It took four men to carry the first hog. It was about 350 pounds dead weight.

Young George had been all eyes while this was going on in the cold early morning dim light of dawn. He said, "Mr. Henry. I miss this old hog cause I fed him since he was a baby pig. We called him 'Oscar'." Mr. Rupp told Young George he could get some new pigs to feed for next year's butchering. With that he cut off Oscar's tail and gave it to Young George.

Grandpa and Papa used their sharp butchering knives to cut open the dead hog. They put the heart, liver, intestines and stomach and other inside parts in an old tub that they carried to the cellar under Grandpa's house. It would be warmer there, and the women could begin to separate what would be kept for cooking and what would be used for lard. The head was saved and

(cont'd)

meat cut off for other by products for the Shaffer family.

One by one, Henry Rupp had readied the hogs to be hung up in the wagon shed. Grandpa had told Henry Rupp to come back the next day to help them cut up the hogs that would be left hanging on the tripod during the cold night.

For the curing work, they rubbed salt, brown sugar, black pepper and salt peter on the meat and would leave it for a month or so in the cold. The smaller items, like spare ribs, heart, liver, tongues and lean sausage meat were put in the cellar on a special table to be cut up later. . The second day Henry and Papa began cutting hams, shoulders, bacon, backbone, loin and other choice pieces of pork to be kept and carried up to the attic tables.

Head butcher and his helper were paid for their work with several pieces of pork meat which was the usual custom for a person who helped butcher. All the trimmings were ground into sausage which was made into cakes, fried down, and put in large crocks and sealed with hot lard poured on top. Scrapple was made from boiled broth made from the head meat, bone meat and meat scraps. It was mixed with corn meal and put in pans and later fried for breakfast.

The small intestines were cleaned, scraped and used for casing for sausage. Some farmers used the stomachs for stuffing meat and potatoes, apples and cabbage for a special roasted butchering celebration. Much of the cured meat would be carried and hung in the old smokehouse for a slow-burning smokey hickory or apple wood fire which added a special flavor to the meat.

The hog carcasses hang from tripods after they've been gutted and cleaned. Now they will be cut up and smoke or salt cured. Hog meat was a mainstay for farm families of the 1800s.

Homemade Lye Soap

"One ritual each year after butchering days on the old farm was making the year's supply of soap. Rarely was such a thing as using sweet smelling store-bought soap for taking a bath or washing dirty clothes. A little lye mixed with fats saved from butchering and the kitchen, along with a little wood ash was generally the farm wife's recipe for a good strong homemade soap."

Grandma taught Mama and the girls how to make soap. She made sure they saved the fats and drippings from the kitchen stove as well as beef tallow and pieces of hog fat as they butchered.

A mixture of water, caustic soda (lye and wood ashes) and fats boiled for several hours was poured in flat old black tins and allowed to cool and dry. It was then cut into squares and stored in the cellar until it was needed.

Chunks of homemade soap kept the clothes and everybody in them clean.

Lye soap was used for dishwashing and washing heavy work clothes and other garments until they were clean. The men could always find a cake or two of Grandma's soap in the wash basins on the benches on the back porch.

Once in awhile Mama would allow the kids to use some sweet smelling store-bought soap for a bath. The girls always liked it because they said it was good for complexions. Young George always teased Helen saying, "Helen you've been reading too many magazines.

A Trip to the Lime Kiln

"Farm crops did not grow well without adequate lime in the soil. The burning of limestone in crudely built kilns was the answer to providing farmers lime for their fields. The burnt limestone was hauled to a farm from the kiln and spread by hand."

Grandpa and Papa were in deep discussion out in the barn one winter afternoon. Young George was rubbing the head of one of the young calves and at the same time listening to what the two farmers were saying. But the word "lime" was new to him. After all, a five-year-old couldn't be expected to know everything about farm life yet.

"It seems the back field didn't give us the best crop of hay last year," Papa said. "Yet we had plenty of rain." And Grandpa replied with some words of wisdom. "You know, we haven't limed that field in about 15 years. I believe that's what it needs. Why don't you ride over to Naylor's lime kiln and see if we can get on his list for burning some lime or getting a delivery of several loads of lime before too long. And take Young George over with you so he can see how lime is made."

Grandpa added, "One of these days old lime kilns will give way to those new-fangled ways of burning and selling limestone."

The next day Papa and Young George hooked up old Bess to the milk wagon and headed up the road to Naylor's lime kiln. Papa had been there several times before and soon found John Naylor at his small stone quarry next door to the kiln. Mr. Naylor rubbed Young George's head and said to Roger, "I see you've got a young farmer over on the farm, huh? What can we do for you?"

"I guess Grandpa and I need a few loads of lime for our back field. I also thought I'd show Young George here how you make lime. Can we go across the road to the kiln before we leave," Roger asked.

Mr. Naylor said they fired the kiln a month ago and still had some burnt lime in the bottom. He said if the fields were still frozen enough for his wagons, he could deliver the lime next week. "How many loads do you want?" Naylor asked. Roger reckoned they had 20 acres in the field.

The lime kiln was usually cut into the side of a hill with the entrance to the stone chimney at the bottom. Limestone, wood and coal were dumped through an opening at the top.

The team is ready to deliver a load of lime from the kiln to a farmer who would hand spread from piles dumped in his fields. Note that the team is controlled by the rider on the mule.

John Naylor told Roger, "You know we sell lime by the bushel basket. That's three feet tall and about two feet wide, and to haul it over to your farm, that would make it 10 cents a bushel on the ground."

After the deal had been made, Papa took Young George over to look at the kiln where Mr. Naylor burned his lime for local farmers. "Young George, you saw Mr. Naylor over in the quarry and his big steam engine he uses to run that stone crusher to break stone into smaller pieces." Papa continued, "That was limestone, and it breaks a lot easier than some stone. He loads the stone on his dump cart and brings it over and dumps it into this ten foot hole that's about 20 feet deep. At the bottom, there's a steel plate which supports the stone and wood. The kiln is usually lined with soapstone that won't crumble with the hot fire. He then drops some of these oak logs on top of the first layer of stone and sometimes coal before he dumps in more limestone. He keeps putting in layers of stone, wood and coal until the kiln is full to the top."

"Down at the bottom," Papa explained, "there's a small tunnel leading into the kiln. It has a metal door that opens and shuts to control the amount of air that goes up through the kiln after Mr. Naylor lights a fire at the bottom. Once all the coal and wood burns for about two weeks, the limestone has turned to small pieces of white lime, and it's then ready to be hauled to the farmer's fields. The mortar between the bricks in Grandpa's house is also made from a mixture of burnt lime and sand."

True to his word, Mr. Naylor had his men start hauling with six-horse wagons loaded with lime to the back field. Young George went over with his Papa to watch the unloading of the lime in small piles about 10 to 20 feet apart. Before the lime was spread by Grandpa, Papa and ole Jeff with shovels, it had to air slack. Grandpa figured it would take all winter to spread the piles.

Papa had already told Young George that this lime would mix with the soil in the field to make the crops grow taller. "Lime is just like food we eat," he said. "Only it's for our crops to eat."

The Big Red Barn

To "raise" a barn, each mammoth frame section was laid out on the ground and the beams of chestnut or white oak were pegged together. Then the gathering of men wielded pike poles to lift and shove and push the sections into place.

"When it came to farms, a farmer considered his barn a most sacred place. It provided a roof over his animals and a place for storage of his crops. Probably the biggest part of his day was spent in the barn, yet it provided a living for him and his family in the 19th and early 20th centuries."

Young George got one of his first lessons on building barns when a freak windstorm blew down the old barn on the Shreck place near the old Valley Railroad station near the Mill. The Shaffers were among 50 or so other farmers who were soon on the scene to help build a new barn for the Schrecks. Many farmers' wives came along to prepare meals for all the helpers.

Building a new barn was not a new experience to most farmers, for they and their fathers had all been to a few "barn raisings". Young George at eight years was seeing his first. It wasn't long after the disastrous windstorm that the chestnut and oak lumber had been cut and sawed at Mr. Wisner's sawmill. Big supporting rafters were laid out on the ground first where they had to be cut, augered for pins, chiseled to strike a mortise and tenon and pinned while on the ground. They were then raised bent by bent (section by section) with human brawn and pike poles on the barn floor after it was in place. The bents were then ready for the rafters and plates. The shingled roof would be completed later by the Shreck family.

It didn't take more than a day for the "barn raising", and for the framing to be tied together. Young George was interested seeing how three or four farmers "knew what they were doing" and seemed to give the orders as each timber was pinned in place. Papa told him that they were "framers" and good carpenters. The thick stone walls were not blown away but the large unsawed beams had to be replaced and spaced for the floor boards to be nailed in place before the "barn raising" started. The flooring was thick enough, and the log beams heavy enough to hold wagons full of hay and mows piled up to the ceiling with hay and straw.

Grandpa told Young George that barns built by German farmers were usually built into the slope facing south and "down over the hill to protect it from the winter winds." He explained it also made it easier to build the dirt bank up to the main floor for the wagons to be pulled into the barns. They were called "bank barns".

Barns were usually painted red with red ochre powder mixed with oil to provide the red color and protect the chestnut boards from the rain and weather. Most had cupolas on top of the barn. Grandpa told Young George because of all the cows and horses in the bottom of the barn, and the hay in the top, there was a lot of moisture. The cupola and louvered windows in the gable ends of the barn help keep the air moving, and the barn siding didn't rot easily.

On the livestock level, the Shaffer's barn had a place for 15 cow stanchions, 8 horse stalls and large entry walkway between. They also had room for pens for the bull and calves. Part of the large barnyard was covered with the barn overhang (forebay) where the heifers could get in out of the weather. All barns had hay lofts and mows on both sides of the wagon entrance, and many had two wagon entrances with two additional mows. Most barns had a grain storage room which the farmer tried to keep "rat proof" even though he usually kept many cats around.

The Seeds of Spring

"Spring was the time when a farmer loved the sweet smell of the newly-turned soil. It was a busy time with plowing and planting, but the farmer was also at the mercy of the weather.

In addition to the multitude of household duties, farm women took care of the garden plot which yielded much of the food supply.

Any farmer who got behind in his spring planting was in trouble for the rest of the year. And if planting season was late because of the weather, a farmer could end up with 20 acres of fodder and no corn.

Grandpa Shaffer faithfully depended on the Old Hagerstown Almanac and the phase of the moon for his weather forecasts and planting schedules. He also taught Roger that the horses and mules were to be well-fed prior to the busy spring work in April, May and June. The animals would have some of their hardest work at this time. A sick or poorly-fed horse or mule could put the spring planting behind schedule.

What plowing the Shaffer farm did in the previous fall was never enough for all the crops that had to be planted. As soon as the ground was dry enough, Grandpa and Papa Roger were in back of the plows after the morning milking and other farm chores had been completed.

Once the ground was plowed, it was harrowed with a spring tooth harrow to break down the clods of earth. After the soil was broken down further with a two-horse roller, it was ready for corn planting—the top priority. Grandpa insisted that seed corn be planted between May 10 and May 15. By that time the spring sun was strong enough to start warming the ground. He was never in a good mood if his corn had not grown to at least waist high by July 4.

(cont'd)

About the time the Shaffer men had finished plowing, Grandma Shaffer and Young George's Mama were on the men's backs to get their two-acre garden ready for planting. True, it had been plowed in the fall, but they insisted it be harrowed and rolled so that there were no large clods that would keep their seed from growing.

The ladies had already received their green bean, peas, corn and other vegetable seed they'd ordered from the new Burpee catalogue. But many of the seeds they used were dried and saved from the previous year. Papa had cut the lima bean poles during the winter. The seed potatoes, peas and cabbage plants had been planted in April. Grandpa and Papa experimented with raising tomatoes for a local cannery around 1900. They planted about five acres of tomato plants they had grown from seed. They wanted to see how a tomato crop would fit in with their normal farm work and whether the money from a cannery was worth the work. The tomato plants had to be planted, cultivated at least three times and hoed to get rid of the weeds. The hardest work would be the picking in August and September. Tomato picking would pull in Mama, the girls and Young George to help. The tomatoes would then have to be hauled to the cannery and unloaded.

The tomato experiment worked for awhile but gave way to planting two acres of green beans for the cannery. This crop was just as hard, so the Shaffers gave up on the experiment. Young George was glad to get rid of those hot tomato and bean picking jobs. He figured going fishing probably would be a much more satisfying way to spend a lot of his summers off from school.

First the ground had to be turned over with a two-horse plow. Then it was harrowed and rolled before the corn seed could be planted.

The Hay Crop

"Horses and cows have to eat. Much of their basic food is hay—grass that is cut, dried, hauled and stored in the barn awaiting to be fed when the pasture's green and lush grasses have been frozen."

School had ended at the beginning of the summer's harvest season. Papa and Grandpa were busy cutting and harvesting hay and would need Young George to help with forking the sweet smelling clover hay into piles after it had been raked. They would then be loading these piles onto the hay wagon.

Loading and unloading hay into the barn's hay mows was not an easy job. Grandpa had to hire two men to help during the hay harvesting and would pay them seventy five cents per day. A large part of the winter's supply of hay was cut in May and June when the first cuttings of clover and timothy hay, if good, assured that the Shaffer hay mows would be at least half full.

Papa was using for the first time the new two-horse four foot iron bar (side-cut) mower that Grandpa bought for fourteen dollars in nearby Pennsylvania. Not only did the hay have to be mowed down, but it had to be raked with the balance dump rake after it had dried laying in the field for a day or so.

Young George finally got a chance this year to help Papa with loading hay. He was able to stay on the hay wagon with his Papa as the two hired men lifted the piles of hay to the wagon where Papa would spread it carefully to make sure that it did not slide off the wagon as the horses were pulling it to the barn.

Young George could stay on the wagon as long as he remained in the middle of the load as the height of the load got higher. As they were riding to the barn, Papa said, "Young George, I want you to hang on to me as the horses and wagon come onto the barn floor. Then I'll help you slide off the wagon before we start forking it over into the hay mow on the left
side of the barn." Young George liked to ride on the wagon. In fact, he reached out and pulled off a yellow summer apple from an orchard tree as they passed by.

Shortly after Papa had taken over much of the harvesting work from Grandpa, he had a harpoon hay fork and trolley system installed in the top of the barn. The fork cost one dollar and thirty cents and the trolley hay carrier cost three dollars and fifty cents. The track installed in the top of the barn to support the trolley cost fifteen cents a foot. The new hay unloading equipment was designed to carry fork loads of hay from the loaded wagon to the top of the barn. The hay was then pulled over a hay mow where it could be dropped below and spread by hand. The new trolley system was powered by "Ole Bess" through a series of pulleys as Young George led her away from the barn while she was pulling a rope leading back to the hay fork.

Papa's new hay unloading system did the work of two or three men that previously loaded and unloaded the hay. Later in the summer, if there had been sufficient rains, the Shaffer's would be cutting the second crop from their hay fields. Some years when there was no early frost, a possible third crop could be cut.

Thrashing Days of Old

"Always on the hottest of summer days, the old thresherman would come into the farm lane at dawn or the night before—his noisy Case steam engine with iron wheels chugging and creeping along about five miles an hour up to a farmer's barn—to thrash his wheat or barley. He expected two good meals in addition to his pay for the day."

Grandpa and Papa always tried to get Orndorff, the "thresherman", from down in the valley to bring his steam engine and threshing machine to the farm as close to July 15 as possible. True, it was the hottest time of the year, but by then some of the neighboring farmers might be free to help load the sheaves of wheat onto the hay wagon and bring it to the barn to be "thrashed".

Mama and Grandma would have a big ham and egg breakfast with hotcakes for Orndorff and his crew. Then they went out to the barn to get the equipment lined up with the strawshed. Once the whirring noise of the thresher reached a certain pitch, Papa and his first wagon load was ready to feed the sheaves of wheat into the thresher, and the bags were hooked up to catch the wheat seed which had been separated from the straw.

Young George was approaching ten years and was put in charge of pushing back the straw from the blower feeding into the strawshed. He liked that job because some of the young neighbor boys could help with that hot, dusty job. Brother Ralph was the waterboy.

(cont'd on p-100)

While one farmhand takes a swig of water, his partner uses a three-finger "cradle" scythe to cut the ripened wheat. It was then gathered and tied into "sheaves" and loaded onto a hay wagon and hauled to the barn. This was in the days before the binder machine.

Pictured is a 19th century threshing machine ready to go to work. The man on the platform feeds wheat sheaves from a wagon into the thresher. Bags are ready to catch the wheat as it is separated from the straw.

The old gasoline engine powers the belt which is connected to the threshing machine. The thresher separates the kernels of wheat from the straw that is blown into the strawshed. Wheat is collected from a chute on the side of the machine.

At noon Young George and his helpers could hear the thresher's high pitched whirring sound slow down, and Papa shouted, "It's dinner time". Mama and Grandma and one or two neighbor women had the harvest dinner ready on two large tables in the yard. There was plenty of ham and cabbage, roast beef, fried chicken, green beans and potatoes with apple and cherry pies for the two dozen or so hungry neighbors and threshermen.

Young George sat with the men and listened to the news about what was happening on the nearby farms. He tried to sit close to Orndorff because he seemed to know most of the news, and his squeaky high voice fascinated him most of all. After the harvest dinner and a one-hour rest, the crew all moved back to the thresher and finished hauling and threshing the wheat which was still left. The job was finished around three in the afternoon, and the neighbors left to do the milking on their own farms.

Grandpa and Papa paid thresherman Orndorff three-and-a-half cents per bushel for his threshing job. Orndorff gave them his schedule for doing the neighbors' threshing. Papa would go help the neighbors who had helped the Shaffers with a day of "shared labor".

Before the threshing machine, wheat was "flailed" or beaten by hand to separate the wheat seed from the straw. Instead of one day with a threshing machine, flailing wheat could take all winter.

Grandpa told Young George this way of threshing wheat was a lot easier than when he first started farming. "Then we had to use the cradle to cut the wheat and only got about an acre cradled each day." Grandpa said. "Once we brought the wheat into the barn, it took most of the winter to use a flail to beat the wheat straw we spread out on the floor. Then we'd scoop up the loose wheat seed into the grain fan for blowing out the chaff. It then went down to the mill for our flour."

Young George had always wondered what those two well-worn sticks were which hung on the granary feed-room wall. It was a flail that Grandpa and his boys had used to beat and separate the wheat from the straw before the threshing machine was available to the farmers.

The sheaves of wheat are loaded onto the hay wagon to be hauled to the thresher.

Cutting the grain was a hot summer job. Sheaves of wheat are cut and stacked by hand (above), while a team of mules pulls a binder (below) as it cuts wheat in early summer. This binder also tied the sheaves to be stacked and then hauled them to the barn. But possibly the hottest job was swinging a scythe to cut wheat or tall grass. Two men head home (right) carrying their scythes after a hot day of work before the binder was available to the farmer.

In the Heat of Summer

Minding the cattle along a stream was one of the most pleasant jobs in the heat of summer.

"To a young boy living on a farm in the early 1900s, summer meant no school, hot weather and a lot of hard work—yet some good times too."

Young George always looked forward to the end of the school year. He was ten now and hoped by the next school year Papa would let him stay home from school to work on the farm until cold weather—and again in the spring when the plowing and planting was done.

Shortly after the last load of hay from the first cutting was put in the barn, the next large farm crops had to be harvested—barley and wheat. The Shaffers had an old binder (one of the first developed which tied the sheaves) they used to cut the grain. It was up to Young George and his Mama and sisters to pick up the sheaves and stack them on end with two sheaves on top to shed the rain until they could be hauled to the barn to await the thresher man. Unfortunately, the work in the wheat field was a hot job just like haymaking.

But to Young George, the most hateful job of the summer was hoeing and thinning corn. True, Papa had used the cultivator between the rows and had gotten most of the weeds. Weeds had a way of growing five times faster than crops, and cultivating did not always get the weeds in the corn rows.
Hoeing was a must. At the same time, there couldn't be more than three stalks of corn growing in each hill, so some small stalks would have to be pulled out to let the others grow.

At the end of a hot summer's day, even a ten-year old's back hurt, and Young George could imagine how much Grandpa's back must hurt. One hot, misty-purplish morning, Young George said, Papa, can I go swimmin' down at Pipe Creek with the neighbor kids?" Papa said, Young George, if we finish hoeing the lower field tomorrow morning, you can go with the kids to the swimming hole tomorrow afternoon. But you have to take one sister along."

(cont'd)

103

The swimming hole was the pleasant part of farm life after a hot day of field work.

Young George thought for a moment about Mildred or Helen going along and quickly replied, "But Papa. Most of the boys swim with no clothes on." Papa didn't reply, so he reckoned Papa meant what he said.

The cornfield was finally finished, and Young George and his sister, Helen, walked the mile through the neighbor's fields to the swimming hole. They had nothing called bathing suits, but Mama had given each of them a pair of old work pants. The neighbor boys scattered for their clothes when they saw Helen coming with Young George.

The water was warm, and they had fun swinging on the old grape vine hanging from a tree, and then dropping into the water. It wasn't much more than four feet deep, but deep enough to cool off on that hot summer afternoon.

Summer didn't bring an end to the usual daily jobs for Young George and his sisters—like feeding the chickens, minding the cows and bringing them to the barn for feeding and milking. Then there was the butter churning, hoeing and weeding the garden. There were wild raspberries and blackberries to pick with Mama and Grandma along the roadside and backfield hedgerows. This would provide the year's jellies and jam.

At the breakfast table, Papa always had a new job for Young George, the girls and little Ralph who had now turned five. In July, it was time for potato digging. Summer moved into August, and Grandpa always said these were the "dog days" and warned them not to go swimming. Papa helped Grandpa's no swimming idea by putting Young George down in the meadow with a hoe cutting out thistles and digging them before they went to seed and spread more thistle next year.

Young George wondered if he'd ever get back to the swimming hole. That afternoon there came a rumble and rush of rain and the loudest banging thunderstorm he had ever seen. Papa worried about the streaked lightning, and what if it hit the barn now full of hay and straw which was very much needed for the coming winter.

The next morning after the storm, Papa said, "Young George, it's too muddy to do anything around the farm, so let's go down to the creek and fish for eels while the water is muddy. Eels bite when the water is muddy, so go over to the barnyard and dig us some fishing worms."

It wasn't long before Young George had the first eel. He had to call Papa to get the eel off his line which was all tangled. They went back to the farm for milking and carried a half dozen good eels for Mama to cook. She said, "You boys skin them. I'll cook them." Somehow they got the greenish-brown skin off the eels.

Work was the order of the day, every day, on the old farm. But there was also time for some lighter moments to "horse around" (left), and time for a cool drink in the stream (above) after a long, hot day working in the fields.

The Farm's Vet

> *"Things like quarantines for hog cholera, lung plagues, foot and mouth disease, etc. presented a challenge for states to encourage the education of more veterinarians to care for large farm animals. Before the coming of the local "vet", it was the blacksmith who doctored or gave advice on horse problems. If there was a vet available, he often had to spend the night at the farm to break a fever or deliver a foal (young horse)."*

Young George came running into the barn one May morning yelling to Papa, "The cow—Susie—she's stretched out in the field and won't get up. It looks like she has a big stomach, and she's groaning."

Papa ran down in the field to see about the trouble. "It looks like she's bloated. Must have eaten too much clover, or maybe she reached through the fence and ate too many fallen apples.

"I'll try to get Dr. Keller over here. In the meantime, I'll go ask Grandpa if he wants to use a 'gagger'."

"What's that," Young George asked. "It's a piece of wood tied in her mouth. She tries to spit it out, and that can help let out some of the air in her stomach," explained Papa.

Grandpa Shaffer was pretty good at delivering a calf or foal that was in trouble. Several times he had to call Doc Keller if one of the cows or horses had the colic or was fevered or having

Some veterinarian procedures haven't changed over the years. Just like a vet of the late 19th Century, this contemporary one can tell a lot about the age and health of this mule by checking his mouth.

trouble while delivering their newborn. He would come in his horse and buggy with a bag full of instruments, pills and powders.

Doc Keller came, and soon had Susie on her feet. He told Young George he would make a good vet some day because he didn't run away and hide while he worked on her. "Many boys would have."

Papa usually got the job of working with the vet, and learned what home remedies he could use to relieve a sick cow or horse. Young George was six when he first watched Papa and Doc

Keller deliver a calf that was having trouble being born. He feared for that young calf's life as he peered into the darkness of the stable to see if it was moving or making a noise.

Cow doctors who called themselves "expert cow doctors" were in existence as early as 1625. They tried many kinds of treatment for farm animals, including "blood letting". There were many German farmers who later tried to treat their animals by following certain superstitions that were practiced by generations before them

For example the "hollow horn" treatment that these farmers followed for saving a "mad" cow was to cut off the horns and stuff the empty cavity in the cow's skull with coal tar and covering the area by tying a rag soaked with kerosene until the affected area healed. This action was supposed to "let the evil out".

The Shaffer family was aware of the "hollow horn" and "cut the tail for the wolf" beliefs, but Grandpa refused to follow some of the actions of his neighbors.

The large animal vet of the 19th century used instruments which were throwbacks to the days when blacksmiths did the animal doctoring. Vets, like physicians, were also their own pharmacist, able to compound many of their medicines "from scratch". However, a variety of prepared, "patent medicines" also aided them in tending their four-legged patients.

107

Corn Harvest—Fall Must

As with much of the farm work 100 years ago, harvesting the corn was also done by hand. A farmer and his wife continues to husk the ears.

"Every year a farmer kept watch on his corn for almost six months—from the day he planted his seed, through the cultivating, hoeing and thinning up through the fall harvest. He watched those blades of corn waving gently in the breezes of summer and fall. It was his most precious commodity—almost an insurance that his cows, horses and other farm animals would survive another year."

Toward the end of September all eyes at the farm looked to the cornfield for signs that corn cutting needed to be started soon. It was one of the most dreaded of farm chores because it was hard work. While there were only twenty-five acres this year to be cut and husked, there remained other farm jobs to be done before winter set in.

Papa and Grandpa liked to start cutting corn before a heavy frost hit. But he really liked to see that those bright yellow ears under the husk were fully grown and had begun to dry.

Young George was eager this year to help cut the tall stalks of corn, but his Mama said, "Young George, you have to go to school, but you can go up to the cornfield when you get home. I told your Papa you could not use the corn knife to cut corn. Maybe he'll let you carry what he cuts and put the stalks into corn shocks."

When Young George got back from school, Grandpa and Papa had made one cutting across the long field. He counted the rows and figured that each of them was cutting four rows of corn. As they cut, they carried an arm load of cut stalks to a shock they were building. As soon as one shock was built, Papa started a new one by crossing and tying together four standing stalks which he called a "buck". When he figured there were enough stalks stacked around the "buck", he tied twine around the shock near the top and again started a new one.

Coming from school, Young George greeted his Papa and Grandpa, "Corn shocks look like rows of soldiers across the field. Can I help cut?" Papa said, "No, siree. You can carry some of the corn stalks and stand them around the new shock Grandpa and I just started."

It usually took about three weeks to finish cutting that field of corn, what with the milking, feeding and doing other chores at the farm each day. The next phase would be husking the dried ears of corn.

Young George liked it when they started husking the corn. When Papa knocked the shock of corn down on the ground, he chased those little grey mice across the field—catching them and putting them in a bucket to take down to Tabby, the cat.

Husking or "shucking" included pulling off each ear from the dried stalk of corn with a "husking peg" slipped on the hand like a glove.

(cont'd)

A "husking peg" slices into and opens up the ear of corn as it's husk is pulled down across the ear.

As if standing watch over the field, rows and rows of corn shocks dry and wait for the husking of another corn harvest.

The corn stalks had to be hauled to the barn to be used for feed and bedding during the winter.

Once they had shucked ears from 25 or 30 stalks, they tied them together in a bundle and stood it up as part of a larger shock that could be hauled to the barn during the winter months for additional feed or bedding.

As soon as Grandpa and Papa had several piles of the golden ears of corn husked and on the ground, Young George and the girls filled the large bushel baskets which were then loaded on the wagon. Before milking time, Papa drove the wagon load of corn down to the wagon shed where he and Grandpa would shovel it off into the corn cribs. Those large yellow ears would be feed for the cattle and horses for the next year. Much of it would be turned through the corn sheller by Young George and his sisters to make chicken feed or be taken to the mill to be ground into corn meal. There wouldn't be much to sell to the miller since the animals would need most of it to be able to give plenty of milk or provide energy to pull the plows and wagons during the next year.

The husked corn is unloaded from the wagon and shoveled into the corn cribs near the barn.

The Tin Lizzie

Proud Ford owners gather for a group photo in the early 1900s.

"While the name 'Tin Lizzie' given to Henry Ford's Model T car did not come into existence until 1908, many motorized carriages had already ushered in a new century of travel. In time, they would be replacing the farmer's horses and mules, and sooner or later every farm family will have one of these contrary contraptions called the 'horseless carriage'. They will line up on the streets of town on Saturday afternoons and evenings and watch the people go by."

By the time Young George started to school, the Shaffer supper table was often a-buzz with stories about their carriages (buggies) being able to run up the road pulled or pushed by a motor rather than a horse like "Ole Bess". Somewhere Papa had found a newspaper in town with a picture of Mr. Henry Ford and his first car built with a motor. It was called a "quadricycle" and looked something like a sleigh or buggy with tires like a bicycle.

Papa surmised, "It'll be a long time before something like this is going to go out across the field pulling a plow. I know that steam engines have been trying to take the place of horses, but very few farmers believe they'll be getting rid of horses or mules for many a year."

One day down at Bittinger's store Young George saw his first "horseless carriage" riding down the dusty road. Sam Bittinger said it was a Stanhope auto and looked much like the old Stanhope buggy.

Young George was fascinated with the idea that automobiles would be running up and down the road soon. "Boy"! he said. "Papa, we could race our best horse against Mr. Ford's car and beat him."

(cont'd)

This is Henry Ford's first "Horseless Carriage", called the "quadricycle" which was built in 1896.

The Stanhope automobile made its appearance locally in 1900.

Little did Young George know that after his sixth birthday in 1900 there would soon be many different kinds of cars being made and that he would soon be seeing up close some of these new automobiles down near one of the mills on one of their wagon trips for feed.

A couple of years later, Young George got his first real close look at one of these "horseless carriages". He had gone to town with Grandpa for some harness parts when he heard a strange sounding "put-put" and "clanging" coming up the street. Someone said, "That's old Doc Hering and his new Model C Ford car." Old Doc stopped and proudly showed off his new car to the crowd which had gathered. He saw Grandpa Shaffer, and said to him, "Is that the boy I delivered out at your farm a few years back?" Grandpa replied, "Yep, and I bet you could make that trip now in less than half the time it took you with that fast horse you had then." Old Doc didn't get away from the Forks in town until he showed everyone the motor under the front seat.

It had to be cranked to start the engine. Young George noticed the lights on the front. Doc said they were electric. He said the rear body was able to be taken off, and a truck bed could take its place. Doc said, "You know, Henry Ford is telling everybody who buys a Ford that he can have any color he wants as long as it's black."

Young George kicked the tires and told Grandpa that they must have air in them. Doc Hering said, "Boy, a veterinarian invented the pneumatic tire in 1889 by constructing a hollow tire and forcing air into the tire with a pump. "I'm supposed to get two more miles per hour faster with this type tire."

Before they had left town, Grandpa bought several newspapers for Young George to read and look at some of the advertisements about farm equipment and perhaps one of the new automobiles that Henry Ford would be selling for $400 in 1905. Anyway, Young George had lots to chatter about that night after seeing his second automobile.

The Horse Trader

"A farmer was often dependent on the old horse trader to bring him a new horse to replace one that had died or was crippled with age. About twice a year he would show up at farms leading four to six horses or mules tied to the back of his buckboard. And he always brought a story about how well each of his horses performed."

Grandpa could almost tell to the day each year when "Windy" Dorsey would come riding in the long farm lane leading every kind of horse flesh that could be found. They would be tied to the back of his slat-bottom buckboard with one usually on each side as well as the horse between the shafts.

Grandpa had long warned "Windy" never to come during the corn harvest time because he and Papa would be too busy to look over his "wares".

"Windy" could be counted on (though not always to his liking) to try and sell horses that would "kick the stars out of the heavens", strike a farmer with his forefeet or wait a year to jump on him. Some would break down, and others would jump any fence built.

Grandpa and Papa were always wary of "Windy" as well as the horses or mules he brought along to sell. There were balkers, windsuckers, cribbers and dumbys that had been struck by lightning. Some were even deaf and would balk going down hills or scare off if they saw an umbrella.

If the Shaffers were in the market for a horse or mule, they had "Windy" put the working harness on a good looking specimen then tie him to a wagon to see if he would rear up or fall back and tear up the wagon. They wanted to see if he would run away with anything that had wheels. Then they asked "Windy" to lead him into a stall in the barn to see if the horse would try to smash him up against the stall or jump on him. "Windy" had proven through the years that he was a horse trader not afraid of the devil or any piece of horseflesh known to man. If he tried to hitch a balker to a piece of farm equipment for a demonstration, he sometimes had to fight the critter or get killed. The horse trader fully knew he would risk his life every day, but usually came out on on top of every confrontation even though it was a battle that ended in a "draw".

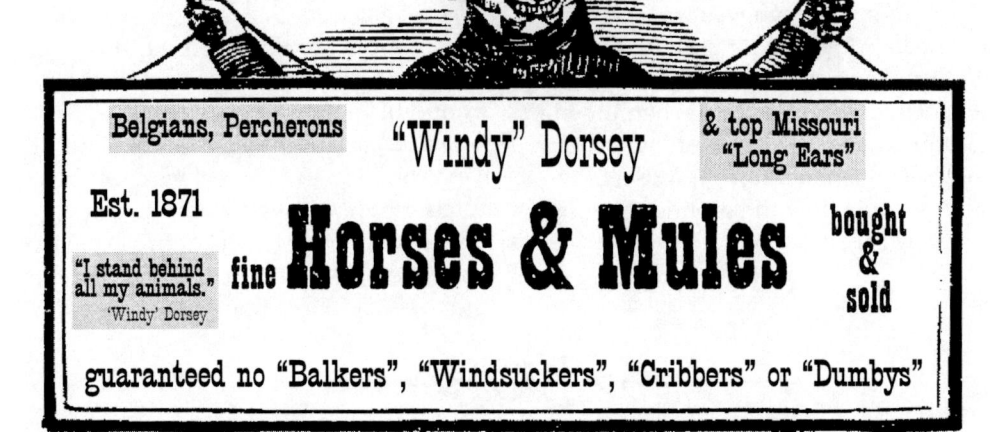

Belgians, Percherons "Windy" Dorsey & top Missouri "Long Ears"

Est. 1871

"I stand behind all my animals." 'Windy' Dorsey

fine **Horses & Mules** bought & sold

guaranteed no "Balkers", "Windsuckers", "Cribbers" or "Dumbys"

The Farmer's Bull

"One of the greatest fears farm kids had was the big, bellowing bull when he got loose in the pasture with the cattle. Rather than cross through the pasture and perhaps enrage him, kids went around it, especially if he seemed mean and protective."

Grandpa always said that a farm wasn't a farm unless it had a bull, a boar and a strawstack.

Nearly every farmer had a bull that served as the father of all the young calves born on the farm each year. It was up to the farmer whether or not the bull was kept in his bull pen in the barn, or chained to a steel post or allowed to graze with the cattle in the pasture. On the Shaffer farm the bull spent most of the time in the bull pen and was allowed to be with the cattle in the pasture when it was time to breed the cattle.

Young George was warned from the time he could toddle until he was well along in school not to hang on the bull's pen or go in the field when the big Holstein bull named "Master" was loose. Young George hated to hear Master bellow or see him paw the ground. He figured he wasn't a happy bull.

Most of the neighboring farmers had bulls they had raised as a bull calf from a good milking cow. It didn't take long before he was bigger and heavier than the cows—usually topping 1200 pounds.

The farm kids usually knew when a neighbor's treacherous bull had gotten through a fence and was roaming the countryside. They usually kept their eye on the closest tree they could climb if the bull showed up. Kids at Young George's school told him never to wear "red" because it would make the bull mad.

Grandpa Shaffer tried to keep a bull with a ring in his nose and a chain around his neck and was usually quiet. If he aged or got mean, Grandpa and Papa sold him to the stockyard or butchershop. Young George soon was able to tell if Master was doing his job. Most every cow had a calf about the time Grandpa and Papa hoped they would.

When Snows Blew

"*It was not unusual for the ground to be covered with snow from Thanksgiving well into February each year. Snow was something farm families learned to live with as a matter of fact. They had sleighs for going to church and bobsleds to haul their milk or get their feed from the mill. Cold winds came with the snow package. The old kitchen wood stove and plenty of dry wood eased the pain of the cold, and the cows and horses had a warm barn and hay to eat.*"

(cont'd)

The bobsled was used to haul feed to and from the mill as well as taking family and church groups for a country sleigh ride.

Young George looked for the first snowstorm each year. He wanted it to hold off until the butchering was done, but if it snowed, he had the runners of his red sled polished and smeared with coal oil (kerosene) to prevent rusting. The hill by the barn was the gathering place for the sleds, and was usually the scene of the season's first ride down to the stream in the pasture bottom.

Somehow, Grandpa could predict a snowy winter. He told Young George, "The squirrels started gathering nuts early this year, and that's a sign of a hard winter. If big snowflakes start to fall, it means the snow will stop very soon. Remember that."

When the first snow came, it was the end of any pasturing of the horses, cows, heifers and calves. It would be the time to toss the dried fodder over the barnyard fence. The fodder had been stacked awaiting the blowing snows and spread around for the day's food for the animals. If the snow wasn't too deep, the cows and horses could find their way to the stream or watering trough below the springhouse for their water. If not, Papa carried water in a barrel from the spring to a barnyard trough.

When the first snowflakes fell, Papa never failed to say, "Young George. It's up to you to make sure Mama has plenty of dry wood, split and stacked in the woodshed. You'd better make sure Grandpa and Grandma have lots of wood ready on their back porch for a monster snow."

Getting ready for snows also involved getting the family sleigh down from its hanging position in the carriage shed. When enough snow was on the ground, it replaced the buggy. Snow usually stayed on the dirt roads, and a sleigh was easy to pull with one horse. The old bobsled frame needed to have the wagon bed unbolted and lifted off the wagon and be bolted in place over the bobsled runners. The bobsled was used to haul milk and also go to the mill when need be. When the snows melted, the wagonbed went back to its rightful place.

The basket sled was light and could be pulled with one horse. It was used to travel to church or town.

Aside from the usual feeding and milking chores, snowy times at the barn provided
the opportunity to load the manure which had piled up in the barnyard. It was hauled to the fields in the new manure spreader the Shaffer family had purchased at the Woodward sale.

Young George despised the job of forking manure. Not only was it smelly, but it was tough on his back to lift the manure that had been wheelbarrowed over the weeks when cleaning the horse and cow stables every day or so. But Grandpa usually said, "Come on boy. We've gotta haul this manure out to the field while the ground is frozen. It will take us four or five days and the job will be done." Young George stayed silent on that assumption.

There was something good, however, in Young George's opinion about snows. The church most always arranged for Papa and another farmer to bring their bobsleds full of straw for a strawride through the countryside. The young people always rode with Papa, while the oldsters got on Mr. King's bobsled to follow. Despite the cold, it seemed warm snuggled in the straw, and especially when they returned to the church for hot drinks and cookies baked for the occasion.

Big snow—little snow—it usually made no great difference to the farm family. If it blew and drifted shut road banks, the farmer used his neighbors' fields to go around the massive drifts. If fences had to be cut, he repaired them before spring. The little snow lasted until the next snowstorm because it stayed cold.

Ready and waiting, the horse and sleigh were the prime means of travel to church or town. Note the sleigh bells ready to jingle.

Young George got great delight in tracking rabbits, coons, foxes and other small animals to see where their dens were. Sometimes he left an apple from the cellar for the rabbit who stayed under the corner of the wagonshed and hidden from his dog, Soybean.

(cont'd)

Daddy's Tracks

Yee las night it snow a heap,
On the level, two feet deep.
Daylight time—or yust before—
I start out to do my chore,
My kid Gus yell—"Me go too,"
I say, "Snow too deep for you,"
But right quick he answer back:
"I can step in daddy's track."
Then his mother pat his head,
"Gude boy, Gus, was all she said,
But I know she thinks lots more,
Ven we start to do dem chore.
Little boys go every day
Vere the old man leads the way.
Better walk straight like a crack,
Ven boys step in daddy's track.

The Country Doctor

Prior to the automobile days, the country doctor traveled and made house calls in a horse and buggy—or sleigh if snowing.

"If someone got sick in a farm family, most wives depended upon their own resources and used old-time home remedies that had been passed down through the years. There were no local hospitals in rural areas. If a doctor had to be summoned because of extreme sickness, someone from the farm had to ride by horseback or wagon to find him. The doctor usually came by horse and buggy and could most often determine through his limited experience what the sickness was. He usually had a pill or a home remedy that would help cure, or at least make the patient feel more comfortable."

The Shaffer family was blessed in that there was very little need to call a doctor. When Roger and Mary's kids were born at the farm, they usually tried to get word to the doctor before their child was born. Young George was the only one of their children who had a doctor present during birth. Their two girls were born when a neighbor midwife was present to help Grandma.

Grandma Shaffer had a good knowledge and collection of home remedies for all kinds of ailments—some of which worked, like bag balm, goose grease, pigeon broth and sassafras tea. Many of her remedies had been passed down from her family though some were from the country doctor who was pretty good at diagnosing a sickness or disease.

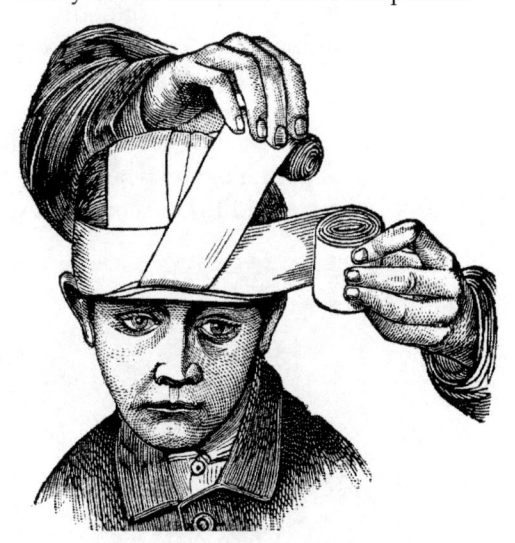

(cont'd)

119

The country doctor, few as there were, maintained an office in town. Behind his office there was a small barn or shed where he could "saddle up" or "hitch up" the old horse to the buggy and head off for his house call.

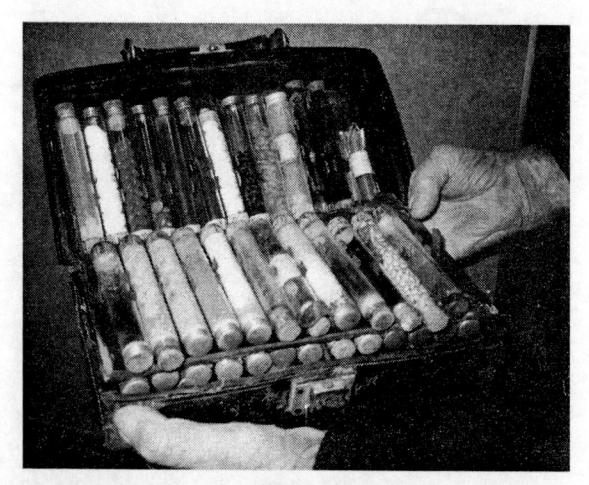

In the country doctor's medicine pouch were pills of all colors which he could prescribe for most any sickness.

Doctors carried their own medicines in their medical bag or small medicine chest from which they mixed the medicines needed for each case. A doctor bought his medicines by the "barrel full" or in large quantities. Aspirin could be purchased in green, pink or white colors. It was often the doctor's child that was given the job of counting the pills for each bottle.

When it came to a farm accident, such as an ox goring or runaway horse, the doctor was called for the emergency, and he brought along his surgical kit. He set many broken bones for which the charge was five dollars. He often was paid with a farmer's sugar cured ham or a sack of potatoes. For his office calls, he was paid one dollar. House calls were $1.50 around 1900, plus twenty five cents a mile costs one way.

Bittingers store, down the road from the Shaffers, also had shelves full of patented linaments, salves, healing powders and tar syrups.

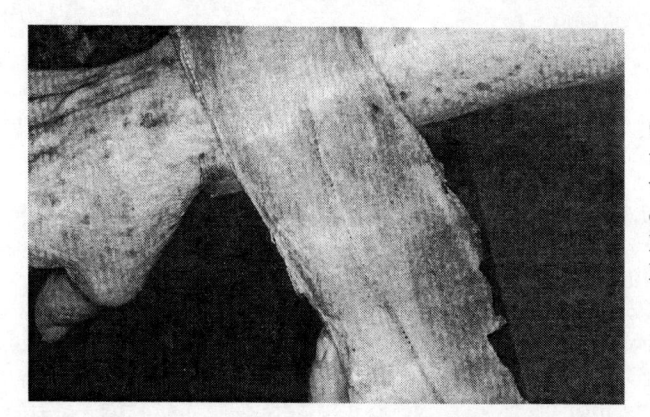

One of the home remedies used for cuts or infections was that of the skin of an eel caught in the month of March—thus known as "the March eel".

Playtime on the Farm

"All work makes Jack a dull boy—is a saying that was pretty easy to come by on the farm. There were times, however, when merry-making had its place as kids found a way to play, far removed from the drudgery of farm work. Whether it was swinging on a rope in the hay loft, fishing on the banks of a stream, skipping flat rocks across the pond, or scooting around the back yard playing 'hide and go seek', play seemed to rejuvenate kids after a day at school or working in the fields or barn."

Young George was a ring leader when it came to play. In no time he had a game lined up for his brother and sisters and perhaps a neighbor or two. There is no doubt he learned more in school about playing than he did about "book learnin".

From the school yard, Young George brought home marbles. He became as good a "shooter" as any after his first year of school. The big boys taught him that "twitches" was a game he could teach and trick others, that is, be left holding a bag on the cold side of the house while the others sneaked into the house and warmed themselves. Other games learned by Young George Shaffer included "quarter ball"—a game like "dodge ball".

Then there was "nip" or kady", "roll the hoop", "pig in the hole","pop goes the weasel", "ante over" and "tree tag".

By far the favorite all-weather excitement was swinging on the hay ropes across from one mow to another in the barn and then drop in the hay or straw. There was also a rope swing hanging on a limb of the maple tree in the yard.

Hoops was a favorite backyard play.

(cont'd)

Sometimes the job of minding the cattle was made easier by the "see-saw".

Sometimes there was time for a pretend wagon train moving across the whole backyard with help from a strange pair of "draft animals".

Occasionally, Papa and Grandpa took their "just-off-the-animal" horseshoes from a nail in the wagon shed and played a game of horseshoes after they had driven two stakes into the ground 40 feet apart. Young George could not toss the horseshoes 40 feet, so Papa let him move closer when he played.

It wasn't long before Young George and the neighbor boys were able to find an old hardball suitable enough to be called a baseball. What rules they had they picked up from the ball games at Backwoods School. The Shaffer pasture field had a fairly level spot to lay out four bases using "cow plops". Papa had cut a stout hickory limb and shaved it to look like a real bat. Usually there were half a dozen boys nearby when word of the ball game got around. Young George would always coax his sisters to play to help chase the balls.

After thrashing, the outside strawstack was Young George's hiding place during "hide and go seek". He would climb up to the top of the stack, hide, and slide down to the ground on the far side away from the "seekers".

For the girls, going to church socials and farm picnics in the woods caught their fancy. They usually took an attractive food box for the boys to bid upon which was the cause for endless giggles from both the young and the old. This frolic was often the beginning of a lasting courtship just as was the "wink" from a pretty young lady in the choir for the benefit of a bashful young man out in the audience.

Around the Shaffer farm, the soft and warm summer evenings sometimes found company visiting on the front porch and the kids in a game of "hide and go seek" amid the firefly hunts and the noises made by the croaking bull frogs down in the pond.

In the fall, the old maple trees provided mountains of leaves for Young George's brother to be covered in. In the dead of winter, the pond usually froze enough for the kids to slide on. On weekends, neighbors brought their skates and there was much merry-making around a big bonfire.

A Hunting We Will Go

"The sport of hunting is centuries old, and all farmers looked forward to a few days hunting on their farms each fall. In addition, hunting provided a meal for the family to enjoy at the dinner table."

Young George was ten years old before his Papa let him go out with the men hunting rabbits. Papa bought him a 20-gauge single barrel shotgun for eight dollars at Bittinger's store. He had been out with Grandpa and Papa before, but always had to walk behind the two as they tramped through the fields and bushes to scare out a sitting rabbit.

No doubt, Young George was excited to be a real hunter. Fortunately, his Papa had him practice shooting at some pigeons as they flew out of the barn.

Papa bought a new "bench-legged" rabbit hound called "Jack". He had already been trained to track and chase rabbits. Young George's old short-legged beagle named "Soybean" worked with Jack who was a much better rabbit dog. He could track rabbits in the briar patches where it was tough walking for the hunter. Jack's reputation as one of the top rabbit hounds in the area got Papa many invitations to hunt with hunters from all around.

The late fall months gave an opportunity for every farmer to find a few spare days to hunt. Sometimes, Mr. Kniple and one of his friends who lived in town drove his buggy out to the Shaffers for a day or two of hunting each season. Usually they were able to shoot ten or more rabbits. Sometimes they were given permission to hunt on the Starner farm next door. Young George went with them if he wasn't in school.

Mama Mary was always ready to cook a rabbit dinner or pot pie, provided the men skinned and cleaned the rabbits in time. If the weather was cold enough, the hunters cleaned their rabbits and hung them up on the side of the wagon shed until Huckster Sam came to the farm that week.

Grandpa had given Young George his wooden box trap to set and get a few extra rabbits to sell to Huckster Sam. He showed Young George how to cut an apple in half, put it in the back of the trap, raise the trap door and set the catch. If the rabbit went in the box for the apple, it would trip the trap door and Young George would have to pull it out of the trap the next morning before going to school.

(cont'd)

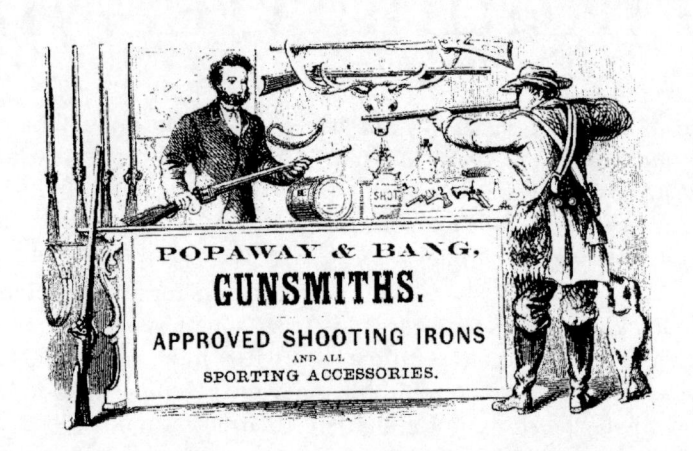

Years ago when Grandpa was younger, he took his steel traps down to the creek and trapped for muskrats. Young George found these old traps up in the top of the woodshed and began to trap for polecats (skunks), raccoons and rabbits. Papa also showed him how to set the traps for the muskrats just outside of their holes in the bank along the stream. During the first week, Young George caught two muskrats and three rabbits. He got ten cents for a rabbit and twenty five cents for a muskrat.

During the fall months Young George took his shotgun into the woods to try his hand at shooting a squirrel. Papa didn't worry about him for he was alone and knew how to use his gun. He got his first squirrel, and Papa gave him a lesson in skinning it for his Mama to cook for his supper that night.

The Old Wooden Pump

A wooden pump draws water up from a shallow well and fills the water trough.

"By 1900 many farmers had hand-dug wells and were pumping water with the old wooden pump, rather than having to walk down to the spring for a bucket of water for the kitchen. It took a good well digger to hand dig a round well pit four feet wide and 20 to 40 feet deep and then line the walls with stone and install a pump."

The Shaffer farm got its water from the springhouse that Grandpa had built just before the Civil War. For the next 40 years Grandpa and the family carried or hauled their water from the springhouse to the house and to the barn. The cattle and horses drank from the old wooden trough down in the field below the springhouse.

Papa figured it was almost time to have running water into the house and barn. First he told Grandpa he wanted to have a well dug near the house so they could soon have an inside bathroom. They'd also be able to have running water in the kitchen.

Once Mr. Mathias, the well man, was hired, along with his helper, Young George watched him use his cherry-forked stick to tell where the underground water stream was running. Mr. Mathias called it his "divining rod" and said to Young George, "Watch how the bottom of this stick twists in my hand. Where it twists the most is where I'll dig the well and find water. We'll strike water down in the ground about 20 feet."

(cont'd)

For one week Mr. Mathias and his man dug the round hole lifting buckets full of dirt up from the bottom of the well. Finally Young George heard him yell, "We got it!" He could see a little stream of muddy water coming in the bottom of the well. And Mr. Mathias began calling for the flat rocks that Papa had hauled in to build the round stone wall around the well sides from the bottom to the top.

Mr. Mathias had arranged for one of Mr. Palmer's wooden pumps with its suction pipe to be set up through the heavy wooden floor on top of the new well. Mr. Mathias told Papa, "We could, of course leave this windlass up that we brought up the dirt with, and Young George could wind up buckets of water for you."

Heavy timbers were sometimes bolted together to create a pump (above) which replaced the old method of lowering a bucket into the well and hauling it back up by cranking a windlass (below).

Papa said, "We might try that for awhile, but I'd rather see Young George on the end of that pump handle pumping our water until someday when we can get a gasoline engine to pump water into the house and barn through some underground pipes."

A Mother's Day

Women pick strawberries in early summer getting ready for another batch of preserves.

> "A farm would hardly be a farm without the labor and love of a mother. She was a housewife who kept the fires burning and the overseer of the money that was needed to pay the mortgage. With her bonnet and long dress she made sure the eggs and butter and chickens were ready for the huckster. She made sure the kids did their share of the farm chores and headed off to school in time, and of course, on thrashing and other big days she made sure there was plenty of meat and potatoes and cabbage, followed with apple pie for all the workers."

It took Young George many years to know how important his Mama and Grandma were in his daily life. As he looked back in that 1900 era of his life on the farm, he suddenly realized these two women were in charge of a lot of important daily chores—probably much more so than his Papa or Grandpa. Nor could Young George do without his sisters, for they, too, performed part of the role that a farm woman did each day.

Little things seemed to be part of a woman's job—like putting wood in the kitchen stove dozens of times each day. Little things included cleaning the soot from lamp chimneys each day. They washed the windows, swept the floors and porches, and washed the milk cans and milk buckets each evening to be sure that the morning milk would be ready to be taken to the community milk stand by Papa. There was no running water, only that carried in buckets from the spring.

And then there were many big jobs the farm woman had a major hand in doing—sometimes by themselves and sometimes with menfolk. It was Mama who had to take the cream off the milk to be stored in crocks in the dark cool cellar or the springhouse to get ready for buttermaking. She had to see that the old butter churn was clean and made ready.

(cont'd)

The girls churned the milk until the butter "broke". Then it was the girls and Mama who worked the buttermilk out of the butter—molded it in neat packages and with a wooden butter print stamp the butter that was wrapped in each package. Young George knew all these jobs, for Mama had him on the churn job many times.

Monday's were Mama's wash days. The clothes lines were full—it meant washing the week's clothes, putting them on the clothesline, taking them down and ironing them with the old sadiron. She was the custodian of the poultry and even spent time milking cows when the menfolk were working in the fields later than usual. Part of Mama's day was having her choice butter, large clean eggs, and chickens or calves ready on Wednesday for Huckster Sam. She collected the money and made sure it went for paying off the farm debts before anything else.

Mama was always in the potato patch, either planting potatoes with the men or helping pick up the new potatoes as they were plowed up to the surface of the ground. It was she who insisted that the large garden be plowed in the early spring, seed planted and vegetables gathered when they were ready.

As the girls grew older, they packed the school lunches and became the baby sitters. They also cleaned the commodes and washed the dishes. They learned quickly to sew on Young George's buttons or darn his socks or put a patch on his pants. They learned how to carry wood before they were of school age. They could pick up potatoes and then prepare part of the evening meal day after day.

Monday was washday. The old wooden tub was used for scrubbing clothes and Saturday night baths.

There were always meals to be cooked, including those for a hired hand or neighbor men and workers during "thrashing" and butchering times.

And of course Mama had to cook Sunday dinner for an occasional visit from the pastor of the church, or relatives who came to get that special Sunday meal and probably carry home some of the farm's choice vegetables or meat.

Mama never got off the farm except maybe once a year to town or to a funeral or to a grange picnic. Mama's day was everyday, seven days a week. The only rest she got was when she was sick or when she "went to bed with the chickens"—which of course she did often.

That White Mule

Grandpa Shaffer was like a lot of other Grandpas. He took a fancy to his energetic grandson—this one being Young George. He had something in mind when he told Papa, "We need a new mule on the farm. I notice you're having to keep old Maude in the barn a lot. She's getting a little old now."

Grandpa continued, "I'm going to look for a new mule, and I want it to be Young George's mule. You can tell him that Grandpa Shaffer is going to give him a mule for his own."

Papa Roger said, "Grandpa. I don't care whether you get Young George his mule, but remember he's only 12 years old. Maybe he'll get hurt playing around with a young mule."

Grandpa said, "Now, Roger. That'll be your problem. You've got to make sure the mule is broken right when we get him. Let Young George get to know him. Have him feed the mule; curry him; talk to him and later, ride him as you lead him across the pasture."

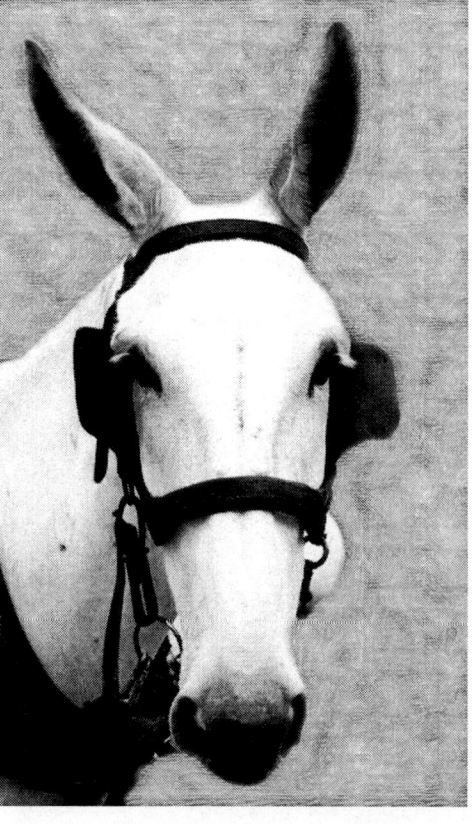

"Every young farm boy, no matter how young or old, yearned to have his own horse—or maybe a calf, cow or pig. It would be his to care for, feed and keep clean as well as having something to brag about at the supper table."

Grandpa said in his pride, "And, oh yes, it's going to be a white mule. I hope that the horse dealer over in Pleasant Valley can get one for us. I'm a little concerned about buying a mule from one of those "drovers" or horse traders who comes around selling horses every once in awhile. They're interested in selling, and then they're gone forever, and we never see them again."

The very next week, Grandpa hooked up the buggy to Old Bess, his prize "church going" horse, and rode over to Pleasant Valley way. Before he left, Grandma had warned him not to get a white mule. She told Grandpa she didn't like white mules.

Luckily he found Jim Frock on his small farm outside the village about noon, and quickly told him he was looking for a good white mule. "Do you know any around for sale." To which Frock said, "No but I'll look around and let you know Mr. Shaffer. I have several brown mules you can pick from.

(cont'd)

Grandpa said, "Jim, this white mule will be for my grandson. He has to be already broken, young and not a black spot on him. Let me know if you find a good one for a reasonable price—around a hundred dollars."

Grandpa got back to the farm at sundown. The milking had been done by Papa, Young George and his Mama. He told Papa he had no luck in finding a white mule.

Somehow, Young George got wind that he would be getting a new mule of his own from Grandpa. He told his schoolmates, and every evening he would ask Grandpa when he got back from school whether his white mule had come. He practiced currying Sam and Jim, Papa's farm mules, always keeping his distance from those dangerous feet that could bear out the saying "kick like a mule".

A month later, Jim Frock came riding into the farm lane in his spring wagon leading a white mule tied to the back of his wagon. Young George was in school, but Grandpa and Papa gathered around Jim to hear about the mule. Jim said, "This mule came from a farm near Gettysburg and he's four years old. He just turned white. You know mules are born black, and this one is just turning white. I've checked his teeth, and the farmer is about right as to age. He's been broken to work with another mule, but I'd be careful if your grandson rides him or is working him alone. Give him a little time, and I believe he is about what you want."

Papa hooked him to an old cultivator to see whether the mule knew his "gees" and "haws" as well as "getty up" and "whoa". Grandpa seemed to like what he saw. Jim Frock continued, "His name, incidentally, is Jack, and I can sell him to you for $110."

Papa came back from the garden and said to Grandpa, "He seems to be quiet and knows when to stop and start. I believe Young George will be a happy kid." Grandpa said, "Jim Frock, we'll try him out and also see how he likes kids. Give me ten days, and if he proves out to be a good, quiet mule, I'll get the $110 to you." Papa was probably as excited about Young George's white mule as Grandpa, and he put Jack in one of the horse stalls. They agreed they'd stay around to see Young George meet his new mule.

Young George came down the farm lane from school with Ralph and Helen and soon had on his work pants heading for the barn. He was set to feed the cows and horses before he filled the wood box. But walking down the entryway, Young George let out a scream, "Oh, boy! My white mule is here!"

Papa and Grandpa appeared, and Papa grabbed Young George by the arm, "Look this is a young mule. He may kick. He may try to mash you up against the stall, or even bite. Let's take it slow and get to know Jack—that's his name."

Young George decided he would feed Jack every night when he fed the horses. He would talk to him, like Grandpa talked to horses. Then he'd brush him off as soon as Papa found out he wasn't a "kicker".

Anyway, he had his new white mule, and the kitchen table would include "mule conversation" before and after Papa's prayer and the word had been given to eat.

Grandma's Funeral

"Funeral customs have varied through the centuries, many relating to the religious beliefs or ones that a country grew to accept with time. For the German Lutherans, burial was held on the third day in keeping with the resurrection of their Lord."

A horse-drawn funeral hearse leads a procession for a 19th century funeral.

Grandma Shaffer became ill when Young George had reached his tenth birthday in 1904. Dr. Hering had indicated to Grandpa that she had reached an age in life when blood vessels hardened and not much could be done to correct that.

Young George was told by his Mama that Grandma was very sick and would be required to remain in bed. Mildred, who was now 16, agreed to move over with Grandpa and Grandma until she got well. She was a good cook, a practice she had learned from Mama. She also proved to be a good caring person.

Every day for a month, Young George stopped over to see Grandma. He would climb the curvy wooden stairway in the cozy red brick house and sit by her bedside to tell her about school and what was going on down in the barn.

Grandma told young George nearly every day, "You are my favorite grandson. Someday, I hope you own our farm and that the Shaffer name will be carried on." Sometimes, Young George took his younger brother Ralph over to talk with Grandma.

Grandma was "called home" very peacefully one night. Mildred, Mama, and Grandpa had been with her as she turned for the worst. Grandpa had tears in his eyes—for he remembered the good times years earlier they had together in buying and trying to make their 90-acre farm one of the best. He remembered her devotion to their church—her faith being unshaken to the very end.

Papa got in touch with the undertaker to come to the farm to make funeral arrangements. Grandpa had contracted for and asked a local cabinetmaker to build a wooden casket made of chestnut boards that he had saved. Grandma's body was prepared for burial by two neighbor ladies and moved downstairs to the darkened parlor room. Papa put a wheat crepe on the door and sent word to the country store and close neighbors that Grandma had died.

(cont'd)

Papa had also arranged for three of the men of the church to dig Grandma's grave. In keeping with the customs of the German Lutheran Church, Grandma was to be buried on the third day. Papa had arranged for several neighbors to sit up with Grandma's body in the parlor. When dawn came, Grandpa came into the parlor and thanked each of them and took them into the kitchen where Mama had prepared a breakfast of eggs, ham and hot cakes. Grandpa and Mama ate with them around the big kitchen table.

On the third day, Mr. Wink, the undertaker, brought in his black horse-drawn hearse for taking Grandma's body to the church and cemetery. Young George had kept busy since Grandma died, yet he broke into tears at the wagonshed when he realized that she would no longer be a part of the happy Shaffer farm and that Grandpa would be all alone. He went to change from his work clothes to be ready to take the buggy ride to church. He would ride with Grandpa and his Mama. One of the neighbors let Papa use his buggy to take the rest of the family up to church.

The minister and his wife came in his buggy to Grandpa's house to give a prayer before Grandma was moved from the parlor. Six neighbors carried her body to the hearse, and soon they all were on their way to the small German Lutheran Church where the Shaffer family had worshiped for many years.

The church was crowded with relatives and neighbors, and the service was simple—as Grandma had requested. As heads were bowed, Young George noted that Grandpa was crying. He too cried lightly, and he hoped Grandpa would be able to get over his sorrow and help Papa with their farming. Already he had heard Mama and Papa discussing how to help Grandpa keep busy so that he could go on as the farmer who was respected in the area. But Grandma would be missed by the entire family. She had been a good Christian wife for Grandpa and a good Grandma for the Shaffer kids.

Grandma's body was followed by a multitude of grieving relatives, friends and neighbors to the grave to be accepted by mother earth to await the call of the resurrection. Young George peered down in the wooden box where Grandma's coffin would be placed.

Grandma had asked that this poem be put on her tombstone—a poem she had cherished for years:

A traditional funeral wreath of wheat is hung on the front door to honor the deceased.

My children dear, by grief oppressed
though in the grave, I am at rest;
my spirit rests with God on high,
where you may meet me by and by.
Rest sweetly on dear mother
thy toils are passed, thy work is done,
and thou are fully blessed,
you've fought the fight, the victory won
and entered into rest.

The family will not continue to mourn alone. For weeks others will come to bring food, help with chores and fill the void for her loss.

The Country Mud Road

A "corduroy road" of logs laid side by side over a stretch of mud made spring travel easier.

> *"One of the miseries of traveling from farm to church or town in March each year was something called the 'spring thaw'. The dirt roads and farm lanes became a quagmire—a muddy mess—almost impossible for the horse or wagon to get through."*

Grandpa and Grandma Shaffer and their son, Roger, and his wife, Mary, lived in an era when getting stuck in the mud was a part of getting to town or church.

When the dirt roads and farm lanes froze during the winter, there was always a penalty to pay—warm weather "unthawed" the roads and no farm wagon or buggy or horses' hooves could escape sinking in 12 or 24 inches of oozing mud. In some places it was deeper.

Farmers along the main roads took turns dragging a homemade log drag which filled in the deep ruts each night before the roads refroze again. Horse and wagon traffic could move better in the early morning after the mud had frozen. By afternoon, the warm spring sun created the same muddy conditions. In many areas, farmers built a "corduroy" road by laying logs side by side in the muddy spots so that wagons could get through.

In the Shaffer's long lane, Papa and Grandpa did what they could to get to the country store or haul their milk.

The main road was usually as muddy as their lane. Papa usually had to do what the mailman did—ride horseback. In those muddy times, buggy wheels took a beating with loosened rims or broken spokes.

Each year the Shaffers and other farmers usually picked up and piled stones along the sides of their fields when the plowing and harrowing was done. In the winter, they gathered up these stones and put them in their farm lanes where the muddy ruts seemed to be bad. After about ten years the lane was not nearly as muddy. But the main roads continued to be almost impassable during the late winter months.

Grandpa and some of the neighbors traveled one day to the county courthouse to talk to the county commissioners about helping to "stone their road". But the commissioners soon found out that farmers who lived on the 500 or so miles of other roads had been making the same requests after one of the worse freezing and thawing periods that winter. The commissioners told Grandpa and his neighbors there was less than 50 miles of "hard" roads in the whole county. They came away from the meeting with only a promise from the commissioners that if Grandpa and those living along the road would haul stone from their woods and fields and place them in their road, and break the large stone with heavy hammers and mauls, the commissioners might find some crushed stone or gravel to put on top.

At supper that night, Grandpa said, "What we needed today at the commissioner's office was a lot of neighbors with those new-fangled gasoline cars I hear about. They could put more pressure on the commissioners and then maybe we could have a good road."

But Grandpa, Papa and their neighbors took the commissioners at their word. For weeks before and between harvests, they loaded their wagons and dropped stone in a trench seven feet wide and ten inches deep in the center of the road. The stone was broken with their heavy mauls. Even then they only stoned about a half mile toward the old toll road leading toward Pennsylvania. The county commissioners, true to their word, did put smaller crushed stone on top of the rough field stone the farmers had laid.

The next year, the farmers in the area figured they would go after another mile or so of stone road. Grandpa said, "Every little bit helps to get out of the mud.

The Telephone Is Born

"It wasn't until a quarter of a century after Alexander Graham Bell talked for the first time to his friend Thomas Watson in 1876 that country folk could start to explore the miracle of daily gossip sessions over the telephone with their neighbors. Even then, some farmers lived too far out from town. Another quarter century passed before enough chestnut telephone poles had been cut and farmers had banded together to form numerous small private telephone companies to serve their farming community."

The first telephone anywhere near the Shaffer farm was on a wall at the Bittinger store. Any farm family who needed a doctor or vet always went to the store where Mr. Bittinger rang the telephone number and let the farmer or his wife do the talking. It was just about 1900 when the private telephone line was built that far out of town.

For those farmers living off this main line, it was usually another group of farmers who formed a new private telephone company that dug holes and installed chestnut poles. It was also probably the youngest farmer who could climb the poles as fast as a cat with tree climbers on that got the job of installing two wires to a glass insulator atop the poles.

Papa Shaffer headed the farmers' private telephone company in his section of the north county. He always let inquisitive Young George tag along in the wagon with the wire and insulators to be put on the twenty foot poles. Of course, most of this work was done between planting and harvest seasons.

Young George would always ask Papa, "Why do you need two wires on every pole?" Papa would reply, "Two wires are needed for each rural line. If someone wanted a private line of their own, then two more wires would have to be added on top of the poles. That would be their cost. Right now we have six farmers who will use this line and maybe more if the line is extended up the road."

The real questions came from Young George as he saw the wooden telephone with a crank, a mouthpiece, a hearing piece hanging on a hook, with two bells being put on Grandpa Shaffer's wall in his kitchen. When the telephone box was opened, he asked, "Why do you need two dry cell batteries?"

Papa would say, "We need one battery to send our voice over the wire and one to receive the caller's voice."

The country phone really became a country phone when the line was up and Young George could call Johnny Yingling's house by turning the crank two short rings. Each farmer had his code—short rings or maybe a long ring and a short. The Shaffer's number was 814F4 which meant four short rings on the 814 line. A long ring by itself would get the operator in town (probably at the switchboard in her home), and she would connect the caller with the doctor or the hardware store if you asked.

Papa collected a dollar and a half each month from farmers connected to the private company's line. This money was used mostly to make line repairs or fix a phone as well as pay the fee to the company that owned the main lines and switchboard. Papa hired someone to do the maintenance work if he or another farmer in the private company did not have time.

Needless to say, every farmer's wife found that the party line furnished the news of what was going on each day—who was having a baby or what the preacher said on Sunday. Many times Grandpa had to tell two of his "talking" neighbors to get off the line so he could make a call. There were very few secrets anymore on a party line with six to ten farmers connected to the same line.

This telephone of the 1890's is one of the first built and installed in country stores and farm houses.

Grandpa Slows Down

"Age has the distinction of requiring a farmer to pull back from his daily routines and laborious work. The family usually covered some of the adversities of old age by advancing the next generations to accept and continue the major responsibilities of running the farm."

Grandpa was feeling better about not being able to lift a forkful of hay after Young George began helping with the plowing and the heavy barn work. He was in his 70s—Grandma had died, and milking the cows was becoming a difficult task.

By this time, Young George was almost 16. He had finally reached his goal of not having to go to school in the spring and fall months when the spring plowing and fall corn harvest needed more than just one hand (Papa's). The brawn of Young George's body was ushering in manhood to where he could easily roll over the plow at each turn and head back across the field.

When Grandma died in 1910, Grandpa moved over into the small house and Papa and Mama and their family moved to the brick house. Grandpa took his meals with Papa and Mama and the kids. But Grandpa refused to call his turning over the farm to Papa a part of something called "retirement". He gladly continued fixing harness, cutting potatoes and absorbing some of the light farm chores, such as currying the horses and mules each day. Occasionally he would haul the milk down to the farmer's milk stand to be taken by others on to the railroad.

Grandpa essentially prepared for Papa's assumption of the farm's ownership. He even reaffirmed Grandma's pledge to Young George that she hoped the farm would be his someday. Papa and Grandpa knew that Grandpa would always be a part of the farm as long as he lived and would not be expected to do more than he was physically able.

Even Young George was there to lift something that Grandpa couldn't. He would say, "Grandpa. You have no business lifting that plow and hurting your back."

A Look to the Future

By the turn of the 1900s, the Industrial Revolution had a strong effect on farming practices. Some of the laborious handwork, such as using pitchforks to handloading a hay wagon (above), was slowly being replaced by implements like the mechanical hay loader pictured on page 140.

> "For any boy on a farm in the early years of the 20th Century, there was something happening that would usher in changes to the old farm. Farm equipment was being improved, and the birth of the tractor and automobile was putting pressures on the dependency of the horse and mule as the sole source of "horsepower". The possibility of a war in Europe was also a concern to America."

Papa was eager to try many of the changes his son was suggesting for improving their farm operation. Here was a 16-year-old kid trying to tell his Grandpa and Papa that things ought to change a little bit. Both Mama and Papa decided to show Young George how much the chickens cost and how much money came from the eggs and an occasional sale of a few chickens to Huckster Sam.

Mama also had the records to show how much they got each year from milk they shipped—the sale of calves or maybe a cow or two. Dairying was the mainstay of most farms in the area. The records Mama came up with showed they didn't get rich off milk or butter sales. Young George told his Papa maybe they should start to raise a couple of bull calves each year and sell them for beef to the town butcher.

At 78, Grandpa watched anxiously from the sidelines as his grandson tried to usher in changes to the old farm's practices. The Shaffers did not get one of the "new-fangled" automobiles to replace their buggy. Young George continued to talk to some of the farm equipment dealers about new lime and fertilizer spreaders and a double riding plow.

(cont'd)

Young George finally persuaded his Papa to buy these two pieces of equipment on the basis that he could contract with neighboring farmers to do some of their custom work when the Shaffers had finished their work.

Fortunately, all these suggestions seemed to work and Papa began to have more confidence that the Shaffer farm would continue to prosper as a result of his son's sound thinking.

Young George's white mule, Jack, had been made the lead in many of their four and six horse teams, Jack had been worked by Young George to where "any contrariness attributed to a mule" was never evident. Of course, Jack was curried and brushed every day by Young George, and when he was fed, he was talked to like a member of the family. He was able at any time Jack was loose in the pasture to walk up and jump on Jack's back and, without halter or bridle, to talk Jack back to the barn.

When it came to tractor talk, Papa was a little slow in wanting to borrow money to buy one. Young George knew that a tractor would soon be in the offing, but was willing to let a year or two go by before he tried to pressure Mama and Papa again. After all, they had agreed to purchase a spreader, double riding plow and a used hay loader. These helped in not having to hire extra farm hands as was the case before the new equipment was purchased.

Young George kept his eye on what was going on at farms in the area. He listened carefully to local farmers as they talked around the potbelly stove down at Bittinger's store. If a new technique or piece of equipment was being used at a neighboring farm, Young George made sure that he and Papa checked it out to see if would work on the Shaffer farm.

Tractor Versus the Horse

The forerunner of John Deere's tractor range was this 1892 Froelich tractor.

"The steam engine made it possible for the railroad to become a reality prior to the mid-1800s. For the farmer, the steam engine brought the threshing machine to his farm each year. Near the close of the 1800s the steam engine manufacturers believed they could build a reputable steam tractor. But the coming of the automobile and its gasoline engine in the early 1900s provided the real impetus for growth of the farm tractor. At least for awhile the horse held its own, but in the years following 1910, it appeared the tractor was here to stay."

As Young George was reaching his teen years, he kept his eye on both the automobile and the tractor. Deep in his heart he hoped that someday the Shaffers would find it possible to own both. Papa, on the other hand, was an interested party, but after looking at the prices, told Young George the horses and mules would, for the time being, have to provide the farm a way to travel, plow their land and harvest their crops.

Young George had read about and then seen Henry Ford's Model K in 1906, and was excited in 1908 when the Model T came to town. There were scores of other cars being manufactured. At the same time, he kept reading about and looking at any new tractor that any farmer had bought. He tried to understand not only the mechanical side of

(cont'd)

new tractors, but how the tractor would fare against his white mule, Jack, and the Shaffer's other teams.

To those manufacturers who thought the steam tractor would take over, the problems with weight and traction in the farm field was a problem. Young George understood that after Orndorff's steam engine got stuck on a rainy summer day when it pulled off the main road. Orndorff explained that the steam engine was designed with a stationary engine to provide power and that for farm work, more power needed to be developed for the steam engine running gear.

Any farmer who bought a tractor in the 1912 era probably did so for the novelty. Most knew little about its operation and less about its repair. The average farmer who was hoping for a tractor, was looking for one suitable for their 80 to 100-acre farm.

Papa didn't object to Young George wanting to learn and understand all he could about tractors. He would say, "Young George, someday you are going to be right about the tractor taking over from our horse and mule power. But I think we may be ten years or so away before our farm can afford a tractor." This set the stage for Young George to study the new tractor development even more as he tried to prove he would be a good farmer."

Ford did some "cannibalizing" to create this 24-horsepower, four-cylinder tractor built in 1904. The rear wheels came from an old grain binder while the front wheels, steering and radiator were off Ford's Model K automobile.

Exit Young George

> *"As a boy grew into manhood on the old family farm, and his play days became a thing of the past, most of the time he settled into the farm routines of his father before him. These could involve taking over the heavy farm chores and may even include looking at the pretty young neighbor girls. Some boys from the farm went to work for other farmers, and a few found a job in town."*

It was the spring of the year at the Shaffers. It meant a year of hard work. Young George, now that he was 18 years old, was now making many of the farm decisions that his Papa had made since Grandpa had slowed down.

Young George had an eye on Esther Wentz, the pretty sixteen-year-old daughter of the Philip Wentz family who lived up the road several miles. He had met her at one of the church socials the summer before. Young George always arranged to take his wagon as he was traveling to the mill past the Wentz farm. Somehow Esther always happened to be working in the garden near the road as Young George came along. These little get togethers soon had Young George borrowing the family buggy and using Jack, his white mule, to make a visit to see Esther each week. In the evenings while talking to his Papa and Mama, Young George would relate to them how lucky they all were to see the many changes that came about in his short 18 years. First there came the telephone that was put in their house in 1900. He saw his first automobile in 1900. Then came the new tractors that were getting more powerful each year by using some of the gasoline engines that were now powering the new automobiles. He recalled for Papa the first airplane he had seen the previous year at the county fair. He said, "Papa, I'm sure I will be flying one of those airplanes before too long."

Young George's early romance gave him more enthusiasm in his quest to see that the Shaffer family buy a new Model T Ford car to help in the farming operations and shorten the time it took to get to town. His argument with Papa and Mama was that the cost had come down from $880 to $550. Henry Ford was now selling several thousand Model T cars each year. The real squeeze came when he kept up the pressure to also buy a tractor. The cost for these early tractors ran about $1200.

(cont'd)

Papa and Mama knew that to keep Young George on the farm, they probably would have to get one or the other. In 1914 they agreed to go the Ford route which pleased Young George since he was now squiring beautiful Esther Wentz.

Other things happened which changed the status of the Shaffer family. Grandpa died in 1912. He was placed beside Grandma in their church cemetery. Then Mildred moved with her husband to another farm in the valley. Helen had married and lived in town. Young Ralph finished Backwoods School and was helping out with the farm work.

The routine at the old Shaffer farm did not really change as Young George was gradually entering into a partnership with his Papa. They planted in the spring—harvested in the summer and cut and husked corn in the fall.

Farm chores continued to be done each day. Young George hoped that some day they could get more land and some of the newer labor saving equipment to increase the farm income each year.

Already most of the people down at Bittinger's store had stopped calling him "Young George"—just "George". He was going to get married, and George reckoned Esther would not want to call him Young George. She probably would rather have their first boy take over a name like that.

There was a marriage and a serenade. Then came a move to the little white house where George was born in 1894. Three generations of Shaffers had enjoyed and made a living on this farm.

Soon there would be another generation—the fourth.

Illustrations

Page T=top, B=bottom, TR=top right, TL=top left, BL=bottom left, BR= bottom right, C=center
cover   "The Haymakers" by Frederick Brehm, U.S. Library of Congress LC USZ 62 44487
frontispiece   Phil Grout
xiii   Phil Grout
xi   ML Grout
introduction   Phil Grout (Louis L. Goldstein)
1   Schwenkfelder Library*
3   (T)   John Huffnagel (B)   Historical Society of Harford County
4   Elmer Myers
6   (T)   U.S. Library of Congress (B) Author's collection
7   by Sarah Brunst
11-12   1897 Sears Roebuck Catalog, Chelsea House Publishing
14   Union Mills Homestead
15   U.S. Library of Congress
16   (T)   Union Mills Homestead (B) Sears catalog, Chelsea House Publishing
17-18   Carroll County Farm Museum
19   (T)   Finch Services (B) Carroll County Farm Museum
21   Jerry Bitzell
22   Rose Hill Manor Park
23   Mr. and Mrs. James Caulford
24   Carroll County Farm Museum
25   Howard Koontz
26   Carroll County Farm Museum
27   (T)   Schwenkfelder Library* (B) Mildred Stine
28   (T)   Sears catalog, Chelsea House Publishing (B) Schwenkfelder Library*
29   (T)   Carroll County Farm Museum
31   Historical Society of Carroll County
33   author's collection
34   (T)   Stanley B. Sutton (B) Nova Development
36   Phil Grout
37   Union Mills Homestead
38   (B)   Carroll County Farm Museum
39   (T)   Nova Development (B)   American Road Builders Association
40   John Huffnagel
41   Historical Society of Harford County
42   John Newman
43   U.S. Library of Congress LC USZ 62-46554
44   (T)   Martin Zimmerman
45   U.S. Library of Congress
46   U.S. Library of Congress LC USZ 62-71132
47   (T)   John Crowl (B)   Carroll County Farm Museum
48   Keystone View Company 138-21576
50   Carroll County Farm Museum
51   (T)   author's collection (BR) John Newman (BL) Martin Zimmerman
52   (T)   Carroll County Farm Museum (C) Helen Totura (BL) Union Mills Homestead (BR) Stanley B. Sutton
53   Union Mills Homestead
54   Schwenkfelder Library*
55   (T)   Union Mills Homestead (B) author's collection
56   Cumberland County (PA) Historical Society
58   author's collection
60   Schwenkfelder Library*
61   Stanley B. Sutton
62   author's collection
63   Schwenkfelder Library*
64   (T)   John Crowl
65   Schwenkfelder Library*
66   author's collection
67   (T)   U.S. Library of Congress LC USZ 62-101317 (B) Schwenkfelder Library*
68   Schwenkfelder Library*
69   ibid.
70   (B)   Carroll County Farm Museum

71	U.S. Library of Congress LC USZ 62-113452
72	Guy Whitson
73	Carroll County Extension Service
75	U.S. Library of Congress LC USZ 62-102047
76, 78	Schwenkfelder Library*
79	Stanley B. Sutton
80	author's collection
81	U.S. Library of Congress LC USZ 62-58576
83	Cumberland County (PA) Historical Society
84	author's collection
86	Mildred Stine
87	Elmer Myers
88	Mildred Stine
89	author's collection
90	Historical Society of Carroll County
91	Schwenkfelder Library*
92	Mildred Stine
93	Phil Grout (Carroll County Farm Museum)
94	U.S. Library of Congress LC USZ 62-51199
95	U.S. Library of Congress
96 (T)	Carroll County Extension Service (B) Elmer Myers
97, 98	author's collection
99 (T)	Keystone View company P175 6216 (B) York (PA) Historical Trust
100	Cumberland County (PA) Historical Society
101	Schwenkfelder Library*
102 (T)	U.S. Library of Congress LC USZ 62-74836 (R) U.S. Library of Congress (B) Cumberland County (PA) Historical Society
103	Schwenkfelder Library*
104	John Grier
105 (T)	U.S. Library of Congress LC USZ 62-113441 (B) Helen Totura
106	Nancy Thompson, "The Good Doctors"
107	Carroll County Farm Museum
108	Schwenkfelder Library*
109 (T)	Dick Bennett (B) Stanley B. Sutton
110 (T)	Elmer Myers (B) Schwenkfelder Library*
111 (T)	Schwenkfelder Library* (B) author's collection
112	John Huffnagel
116	Helen Totura
117 (T)	Carroll County Farm Museum (B) Helen Totura
118	Stanley B. Sutton
119	Historical Society of Carroll County
120 (T)	Martin Zimmerman (B) Mildred Stine
121 (T)`	Carroll County Farm Museum (B) Schwenkfelder Library*
122	U.S. Library of Congress LC USZ 62-123080
123	author's collection
125	U.S. Library of Congress LC USZ 62-44473
126, 127	Schwenkfelder Library*
128	Carroll County Farm Museum
129, 131	author's collection
132	Mildred Stine
134	American Road Builders Association
136	U.S. Library of Congress LC USZ 62-54891
137 (B)	Martin Zimmerman
138	U.S. Library of Congress LC USZ 62-45627
139	U.S. Library of Congress LC USZ 62-58354
140	Cumberland County (PA) Historical Society
141, 142	Carroll County Farm Museum
op. 148	U.S. Library of Congress LC USZ 62-113454

*Photograph by H. Winslow Fegley from the collection of the Schwenkfelder Library and Heritage Center, Pennsburg, PA

Unless otherwise noted, all engravings and woodcuts are from the Art Explosion collection by Nova Development.

I am a retired farmer now 101 years of age. The new book written by George Grier calls it like it was when I was a boy. I was there 100 years ago, and am glad he put many of the old farm stories in writing.
           G. Rodney Haines
           Frizzelburg, Maryland

Hopefully, the school systems see this book as a valuable tool in reliving a part of our history back a century ago, especially our farm heritage for which our family was privileged to be a part of.
           Senator Charles Smelser
           former State Senator
           Frederick and Carroll Counties

There may have been other books written about old farm life. This one has so ably portrayed the life styles our parents and grandparents knew. The pictures are excellent.
           Henry S. Holloway
           Darlington, Maryland
           past president, Maryland Farm Bureau

As a 4-H club member, I feel that Mr. Grier's book on the Old Family Farm gives you a glimpse of what life was like 100 years ago. It reminds us of our humble beginnings and teaches us of the importance of hard work.
           Jenny Lippy
           Carroll County
           4-H Club member

The Old Family Farm by George Grier does a great job of highlighting what our forefathers endured in bringing to us the quality of life which we so richly enjoy today.
           Lewis R. Riley
           Wicomico County
           retired Maryland Secretary of Agriculture

This story enriches the memories we have of our relatives who lived in rural Carroll County, Maryland in the 1800s and early 1900s. This should be required reading for our grandchildren. Thanks for these memories.
           Donald and Leona Dell
           farmer, county commissioner
           American Farm Bureau Womens Committee

Sometimes we forget how our ancestors lived before we had the convenience of telephones, electricity, radio, television, automobiles and tractors. The Grier book has done a great job telling us that life on the farm 100 years ago was not always easy.
C. William "Bill" Knill
Mt. Airy, Maryland   past president, Maryland Farm Bureau

As the Carroll County Farm Museum enters its 35th Anniversary year, education has become a primary focus. The book The Old Family Farm captures the life story of a boy growing up on a farm 100 years ago, using the technology of the time. This book will capture the interest of audiences, young and old, and provide a chance to reminisce and educate.
Dottie Freeman
Administrator
Carroll County Farm Museum

I believe that George Grier has captured most of those activities on the old farm at the turn of the last century. I recommend it highly as part of your reading schedule.
Albin O. Kuhn
farmer and former Chancellor
the University of Maryland

As a farmer's wife for 55 years, I think it is important that coming generations understand what an old farm was like in the 1900 era. This book is just what is needed to tell about farm life 100 years ago.
Jane Smith
past chairperson, Frederick County
Farm Bureau Women

What a pleasure to read this book with clearly and cleverly written short stories about all phases of country life 100 years ago. While fiction, the true to life characters are a pleasure to get to know. The book has brought real hard work and rewards of farming to a new generation of citizens.
Judith A. Stuart
Extension Director
Carroll County

Having farmed all my life, I can really relate to George Grier's book that takes us back to many experiences that we all enjoy revisiting.
James Clark, Jr.
farmer, soldier, legislator
Ellicott City, Maryland

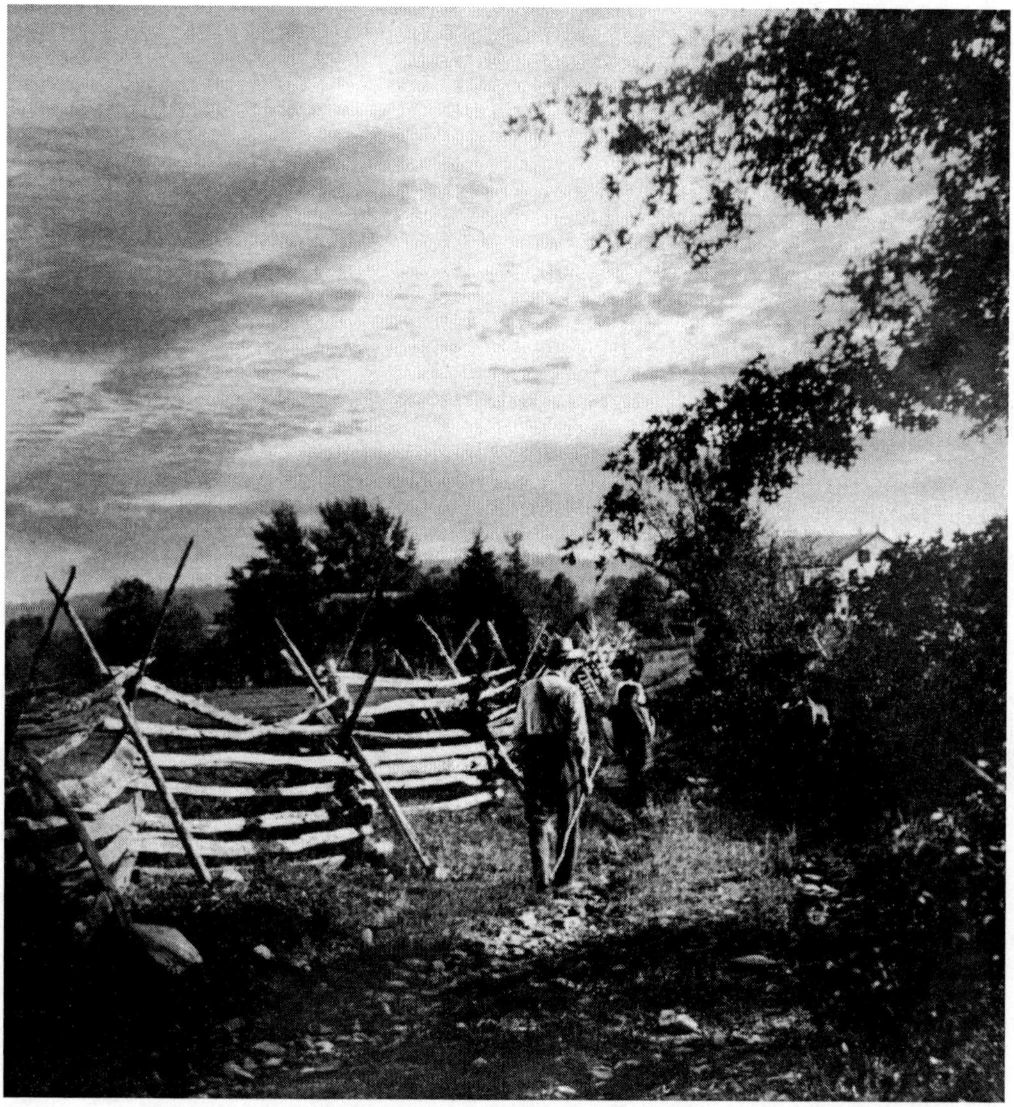

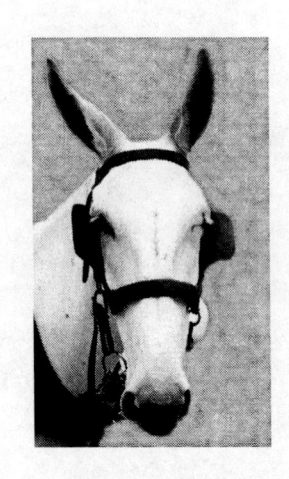